D1260822

TO HELL WITH HEDDA!

To Hell
with Hedda

CARYL BRAHMS
&
S. J. SIMON

London
MICHAEL JOSEPH

First published by
MICHAEL JOSEPH LTD.
26 Bloomsbury Street
London W.C.1
DECEMBER 1947
SECOND IMPRESSION APRIL 1965

Printed in Great Britain by
The Hollen Street Press Limited
London W.1

TO OUR ENEMIES

To show we don't forgive them

CONTENTS

To Hell with Hedda !

[i]

'NO,' said the Boss with great determination. 'Not ninepence.'

'Oh, Boss,' said the man in the muffler, 'think of the over'ead!' But he said it without any great hope that the Boss would. 'We charged a bob at Blackpool,' he argued. 'Packed out, we was. On Bank Holiday,' he added, honesty getting the better of him.

'This is Hoy Haven,' said the Boss, 'and Hoy Haven stands for value for money.' He said it very simply, not as a boast nor as a creed, but as he had been saying it now for fifty-five years. 'And I'm not going to have the public pay ninepence for that.' He waved a hand at the animal orchestra playing wheezily outside the entrance to Wonderland. 'The hippopotamus needs a bit of oil, Joe,' he commented.

'But the nippers love it, Boss,' said the man in the muffler, whose name was Alf.

'I daresay they do, Joe,' said the Boss. 'I don't say they don't. It's a pretty little ride, Joe—what there is of it. But'— he patted the swan that acted as engine to the train of bright red benches—'I timed your trip just now, and how long do you think it took? Two minutes by the stop watch. And that's not enough for ninepence, Joe—not at Hoy Haven.'

9

'I could make the swan go slower,' said the man in the muffler.

'It crawls, anyway,' said the Boss. He jammed on his high hard bowler hat. 'Sixpence admission and not a penny more,' he pronounced, 'and see to it that your dwarfs have their hammers working. Good morning to you.'

The hippopotamus wheezed after him as he strode out into the cold sunlight, the only spender in the fun fair, and at the sight of him the stall-holders in the emptiness around leapt into ingratiating activity.

'Here comes the Boss,' said Three-darts-for-twopence to Four-rings-for-threepence.

'Four rings,' said the Boss. He plonked down his three-pence.

'Free to you, Boss,' said the Slicker in charge of the Houp-la, glibly.

The Boss peered at him. 'You're new here, my lad, aren't you?' he asked.

'Yes, Boss,' said the Slicker. He looked a little less slick.

'Then see here, Joe,' said the Boss, 'Hoy Haven is value for money, and you can't judge the value of threepence, son, till you've spent it for yourself. Four rings,' he reiterated.

The Slicker passed them up. His name was Sid. The Boss pondered the lay-out. Then, with a practised hand, he threw at an egg cup. The hoop circled it, hesitated, and settled neatly round the wooden block on which the egg cup stood.

'Nice work, Boss,' said the Slicker. He passed up the egg cup. To his slight annoyance the Boss took it. 'Shaped like a chicken,' he said approvingly as he stowed it away.

The Boss took aim again. The ring made for a cigarette-case set well in the centre of the stall. The Slicker relaxed.

The ring circled the cigarette-case, enveloped it, wobbled a little, and failed to lie flat.

'Oh, hard lines, Boss,' said the Slicker sympathetically.

But the Boss was frowning. Then he levered himself heavily, steadily, relentlessly over the barrier, stretched out a massive hand and tried to fit the ring around the block. It didn't. He lifted the ring and tried to fit it round a block with a packet of Woodbines on it. It did.

'Good thing the customers can't do that,' said the Slicker warily. 'Ha ha.'

Slowly, silently, awfully, the Boss levered himself back.

'It's your first time in Hoy Haven, Joe,' he said, 'isn't it?'

'Yes, Boss,' said the Slicker, looking as though his hair had been ruffled.

'Well, it's your last,' said the Boss. 'If you're not out of here by morning, you won't be anywhere else by night.'

The Slicker rallied himself.

'You can't do that to me,' he yapped. 'I got a contract, ain't I?'

The Boss shook his head gently.

'You can't have read it, Joe,' he said. 'Clause 17 D.'

He trudged off through the cold morning sunshine in the direction of those damned, flimsy, stomach-turning flying boats.

'Shyster,' said Three-darts-for-twopence virtuously.

Now the Boss was steadily, heavily, unflinchingly levering himself into a flying boat and presently he was circling in it, round and round, wider and wider, his bowler hat firm on his head, his umbrella a sentinel in front, looking into nothing. And as he circled the stall-holders around gazed up at him and marvelled and admired.

'Wonderful old boy,' they said. 'Blast him.'

The swings slowed. The Wonderful Old Boy clambered out, looking pretty grim.

'Three minutes, Joe,' he said. 'You were giving them four last year.'

'So I am this year, Boss,' piped up Joe, whose name was George. 'But I thought you was looking a bit green, Boss, and . . .' His voice died away at the glare that was focussed on him.

'Well, don't think again, Joe,' said the Boss. 'I paid my sixpence didn't I? By rights you owe me three ha'pence of it.'

But even as Joe fumbled, he stumped away.

The Roundabout didn't turn his stomach much. Swirling down the chute of the Chinese Laundry didn't perturb him in the least. But the hard bumping of the Whip tired the old boy so that he cheated a little in the Hall of Mirrors and didn't study his contours in every distorted reflection. At eighty he knew it all. What's more, he knew every thrill, chill and rib-tickler in Hoy Haven—and every trick of the trade they could think up when they thought he wasn't looking, to separate the customer from his money.

Oversize wooden blocks! Ridiculous! Must think he was getting old.

None the less, and he had to admit it, it was beginning to be a strain going round this Fun Fair of his every year the day before the opening, and trying every attraction for himself—just in case it was a little less attractive than when he had tried it last—and making it his business to see that once again it was a fair return for money spent.

'There wasn't much wind in that passage, Joe,' he said as he emerged rock-like from the Haunted House. 'Not

enough to blow the lasses' skirts up. You'll have to do
something about that wind machine of yours.'

'Sure, Boss,' said Tom, resigned. It meant new piston
rings, but there was no arguing, and he knew it.

The Boss passed on. Soon he was looking distastefully at
the Big Wheel. Wonderful value for money—all the same
he longed to let himself off. No fun hanging upside down
at his age, and last year his bowler hat had come off at that.
He rammed it down. No shirking! He looked at the Big
Wheel again. 'After lunch,' he decided.

And now he brightened for the first time that morning.
For he had arrived at his new attraction, the first since the
war, erected through a tangle of God knows how many
forms, and how he got the timber was his own affair. He
hoped. The Wonder of the World with the last nail ham-
mered in only yesterday. The Leaning Tower of Pisa.
Admission One Shilling, Children Half Price. And it was
better than Pisa, for it didn't have to wait for a wind to
start swaying.

'We beat 'em to it this time, Joe,' he boasted to the brand
new Corsican Bandit (21 coupons). 'There isn't another like
it in the world, not even in Blackpool.'

'There is in Pisa,' said the Bandit.

'Who goes to Pisa,' said the Boss crossly. He plonked
down his shilling and started to trudge.

The Boss stood on the top of the Leaning Tower of Pisa,
not swaying yet, and looked with approval at Hoy spread-
ing out around him. The three piers pointing out from the
shore. There they were—one, two, three. There was a
fourth pier but it didn't belong to him, so the Boss ignored
it, even though he knew full well that later on in the season

he would feel a pang of exasperation every time he saw someone paying twopence to go on it. The West Pier wasn't nearly the value for twopence that Palace, Central and Hoy Haven were. For one thing it was shorter than any of the three, and even at that they had the gall to charge for the extension. And the equipment and the slot-machines were even more out-of-date than his own—and that was saying something.

The Boss swivelled inland. The Winter Garden! Now there was a place for you! Plush seats in the theatre, free dancing in the Hollywood café, a separate ballroom for Masonics, and the Louis Quinze Grill. The Glass Dome was shining in the morning sun. Fine view up here. People were going to like Pisa.

The Red Mill. The Boss frowned. There must have been a better place to put it than that. The Eiffel Tower. Blackpool had one too, and—it had to be faced—just as high. But Blackpool hadn't got a Palace of Art, now had it? He focussed to locate it, squeezed between his Palace Pier Hotel and his Hippodrome, East Parade. There it was, the blasted thing—empty as usual. Come Saturday, and the little strip of dazzling white pavement would be milling with people, but none of them would be going into the Palace of Art, you could bet your boots on that.

He switched to pleasanter vistas, the vast factory of entertainment spread out around him. The Shopping Centre! And who leased more than half the shops in it? And who had thought of calling it Fifth Avenue? The peppering of cinemas of all sizes from the giant Paramount to the wheezy de Luxe—have to scrap that one soon. The Music Halls— two more than at Blackpool. Pity he didn't own the Alhambra. What about repeating his offer? Old Caffin must be getting on. Seventy-two if he was a day—and that young nephew who wanted to be an artist!

The snort brought the Boss to the Aquarium—or should have. Where was it now? His Aquarium! Come and see the Wonders of the Deep. Where were they? Panic hit the Boss' heart while his eyes searched frantically among the distant bricks and plaster, huddled together in shapeless abandon. Ah, there it was of course—still there. The Boss drew a deep breath, left Hoy Town and came comfortably to Hoy Haven. The Pleasure Beach where it was a pleasure to spend, started sixty years ago with a modest roundabout on the first plot of land he had ever bought in his life, and everyone telling him he was crazy not to stick to the café and go on saving rent by living on the premises.

And look at it now! No single form of discomfort that could be endured by the human frame missing. You could be thrown up, hurled down, whirled round, jerked sideways and bounced about to your heart's content, and never more than a shilling a missed heart's beat. Sixpence for the Water Chute—tarpaulin and all. Real value for money that was. He hadn't been on the blasted thing yet. Ah well—after lunch.

The foreshore. His bit of sea. Not precisely his, perhaps, but his Skylarks plied on it. There they were, I, II, III, up on the shingle, and IV being repainted—should have been here a week ago. He'd have a word with Joe about that—what was his name now? And what was that whelk stall doing on the Pier Parade? There wasn't a whelk stall on the Pier Parade. Camera Obscura, Palmistry, and a Fun Fair, yes, but no whelks! Why no whelks? People enjoyed whelks just as much on a pier as off it. Wait a minute. Someone had said that to him only last week. That Joe who had talked him into having it. 'Ten per cent. of the gross and I'll make your fortune, Boss.' Well, let's hope he'd do it.

The Boss pulled out his binoculars and ran his eyes along the Victorian skeleton of the best beloved of his three piers. His first pier. The skating rink like a hollow glass wedding cake. The breezy promenade leading to the wind-screened band-stand—nice for invalids. The skittle alley, slung like an undercarriage—one thing about skittles, however much you knocked 'em down you never wore 'em out. Then the Pierrots in the glazed Winter Garden at the end—Merrivale, they seemed to be calling themselves this year. And the extension, free to all. You could catch fish at the end of it if you had the time and the patience. He'd seen 'em do it.

Now what sort of a diving attraction had they got this year? Time was when he used to attend to all these matters himself, and what's more see 'em dive before he took 'em on—after that summer of 1907. But of late there had been too much for one pair of legs, and he'd had to leave more and more to Joe—good fellow, Thomas Bagwash. A little apt to take too much on himself instead of consulting wiser heads, but that's what came of being fifty. You had to make allowances.

Merrivale. Something to look forward to. . . .

Swaying and clinging to the iron banisters like any cash customer, the Boss trudged his way down the Tower of Pisa, loosened his bowler hat and went home to lunch.

'My God,' said Antony Crispin, peering at himself between the messages scrawled in grease paint on his dressing-room mirror. They were supposed to remind him of something. 'I wish it was to-morrow.'

'Pass the powder,' said Wilfrid Wilbraham.

He reached for it himself, dabbed vigorously, stuck a beard over his own hairless chin, combed it out, deepened two lines with grease paint and stared distrustfully at the result.

'How do I look?' he asked.

'Wonderful,' said Antony. 'Every day of twenty-one.'

'Christ,' said Wilfrid. He thickened another line. 'Any better?' he asked.

Antony Crispin didn't even look. He was too busy peering into the mirror, patting.

'Ah well,' said Wilfrid Wilbraham, 'Gielgud's feeling worse than I am. More to lose,' he comforted himself. 'Meant to send a wire,' he remembered.

'Sent mine,' said Antony Crispin virtuously.

'Don't know how you can afford all those first-night wires you send. Not to mention signing them "Tony" so that nobody has any idea which one you are.'

'It helps,' said Antony Crispin. 'Like lunching at the Ivy.'

'I wonder if you're right,' said Wilfrid worried. He smoothed out his beard. 'By God, I'm in a state.'

'John's always in a state on a first night,' said Antony. 'His voice went up an octave in Oberon.'

'Did it now?' said Wilfrid, not much comforted.

Silence settled in the dressing-room of the covered

concert hall on the end of the Boss' favourite pier at Hoy—a happier silence. Nerves, be it the first night of a London season, or a Monday night at any local rep. from Bristol to Dundee, nerves were the order of the day. Gielgud had nerves. Guiness had nerves. Olivier tore himself to pieces. If you didn't have nerves you weren't an artist and it didn't matter where you happened to be having them. And if you weren't an artist you shouldn't be in the theatre—no matter where the theatre was.

There was a knock at the door. Tassel Trevillion came in. She had protruding eyes and a receding chin. She wore paint-stained slacks and a polo sweater. She was assistant stage manager, wardrobe manager, manager, to the Merrivale Repertory Players. She was shivering all over. Clearly she had a right to be in the theatre.

'Now what's up with you, Tass?' asked Antony.

'Nerves,' said Tass, and sat down very suddenly on the trestle table. 'They've gone to my stomach.'

'But you're on the book,' objected Antony. 'You can't fluff.'

'I can be on the wrong page, can't I?' said Tass.

'And how you can,' said Wilfrid feelingly, remembering the dilemma she had got the doctor into.

'Oh, stop nagging,' said Tass. 'I apologized, didn't I? And anyway the audience didn't notice anything.'

'What there was of it,' said Wilfrid.

Tass changed the subject. 'They say,' she announced, 'Bill Bluebird will be down this week.'

The effect on Antony was immediate.

'Think he'll be in to see me?' he asked.

'Why should he?' said Wilfrid.

'I like Bill,' said Antony largely. 'He was charming to me

when I didn't get that part in that play that never got to Swiss Cottage. He said he was sorry that I wasn't quite right for the part. He said he'd have it rewritten for me if only there was time. He promised to bear me in mind for the very next thing he did.'

'But he didn't,' said Wilfrid.

'Bill Bluebird is an awfully busy person,' said Antony, 'but he'll keep his word, Wilfy. Don't worry.'

'Who's worrying?' said Wilfrid Wilbraham on edge. 'What's the house going to be like to-night?' he tenter-hooked. 'Lousy,' he answered himself.

'What's the advance booking, Tass?' asked Tony.

'Two pounds seventeen and ninepence,' said Tass. 'Up on last Monday,' she pointed out.

They brightened. 'It's a good sign,' they agreed.

In the empty foyer of the covered concert hall, a young genius in need of a hair-cut was burning up. Peter Merrivale was cursing Hoy. There it was, the industry of pleasure. Thousands of people spending, spending spending! An avalanche of coppers.

He looked at the drowsy girl in the box office. A whelk stall did more business than he did. Sixty pounds in the bank! What was the use of a small get-out if you couldn't get it in. 'We shan't play to less than eighty a week,' they had assured each other over Soho lunches. Wouldn't they, by God!

A slot machine took more money than the Merrivale Rep. 'Kick a Goal and Get Your Penny Back.' Tcha!

That avalanche of coppers flowing from hand to hand. Placed end to end they would reach from Shaftesbury Avenue to Hell. 'Kick a Goal and Get Your Penny Back.'

There was a business for you. No overheads and a hundred per cent. profit every time you didn't.

Have to paper the house when Bill Bluebird came down. If he came down. Even if it was all landladies. If they'd come. His own had said 'Fancy' when he told her he was on the pier, but she hadn't been yet.

A man and a girl came strolling through the sunset towards the concert hall. They came very slowly, pausing every now and then to look in the water. Casuals, arm in arm, ripe for easy laughter. If he'd been a Palace of Fun they'd be as good as inside already. Still they had stopped to look at the posters—that was something. Unobtrusively, Peter Merrivale edged closer to test public reaction.

'Last year,' said the girl sadly, 'it was the Pierrots.'

They wandered on.

'Nitwits,' thought Peter Merrivale. 'What do they care about Culture. 'Kick a Goal and Get Your Penny Back!' That was their dish.

He strode to the slot machine and glared at the footballers. Toys for Trippers! That's what Culture had to compete against at Hoy Haven. 'Kick a Goal.' It didn't look so difficult.

In a fury he inserted a penny and kicked.

Blast!

He tried again. Oh, good shot, sir!

'I say,' said Peter Merrivale a few minutes later to the drowsy girl in the box office. 'Give me six coppers, will you?'

Past Fairyland, past the Helter Skelter, past Marine Arcade, past the Grand Arcade, past the Victory Arcade, past the Red Mill (they shouldn't have put it there), came

the Boss. On his left the sea and the sunset (free) spread out
before him like a carpet of spun gold. He ignored them.
On his right were all the naphtha flares in the world, and
under each of them a voice, shouting wheedling, huckster-
ing. A never-ending pleasure emporium with nothing under
the counter. All goods on display and all prices firmly
marked—in coppers.

They'd better be.

It was a cardinal rule of Hoy Haven. A wash and brush up
and clean towel cost 2d. on the Pier and 3d. at the Louis
Quinze, but you knew it in each case before you turned the
tap on—if you could read.

Goods on the counter. 'Jellied eels—they're lovely.'
'Sugar beards, fourpence. Be an old man before your time.'
'Come right inside lady and have a look round. Won't cost
you nothink to look.'

Voices selling—selling—selling.

The Boss heard every one.

Past the oyster stalls, past Hoy Haven Rock, past the
lemonades and waffles, past the whelks, past . . . The Boss
stopped abruptly.

'And since when, Joe,' he asked, 'have you been charging
ninepence for ices?'

'It's the cream, Boss,' said Alfie hopefully.

'Cream!' said the Boss. 'Who do you think you're talking
to? Be at my office to-morrow, Joe, and we'll go into the
price of this "cream" of yours. Good night to you.'

Past the Hippodrome—be better when George Formby
got down. Past Bob Hope—quite a queue. Why doesn't he
make me laugh? Past the Leaning Tower—pretty. And so
to his favourite pier.

Waving aside an ingratiating whelk saucer, the Boss

plonked down twopence and strode sturdily along the sunset.

Good to see the young couples, strolling around, breathing in the good Hoy air and spending their money out of doors on good clean pleasures. Many of these boys and girls walking out on his pier would be getting married later. That pair for a cert—look at the way he was looking at her. The Boss wondered how many marriages his favourite pier had been responsible for. He remembered wondering about that to his missus the year before she passed over. Martha had said 'Yes, dear.' He missed her in the evenings.

Not many people going to the pierrots. Couldn't see any kids hanging around. Couldn't hear laughter. Couldn't hear music. What was up?

The Boss made for the drowsy girl in the Box Office.

'Six shillings!' he said unbelievingly. She gathered they'd better be good.

Breathing heavily, squeaking at the soles, and scowling into the darkness, the Boss groped his way to his seat, and fumbled with his hat, his stick and his programme.

'Sssh,' said a solitary addict two rows away.

Not very lively, these Pierrots.

The Boss turned his eyes to the stage. In an old-fashioned drawing-room, two old-fashioned ladies were addressing an old-fashioned young-looking old gentleman.

'He's been here a week already,' one of the ladies was saying. 'Just fancy, a whole week. In this terrible town alone. With so many temptations on all sides.'

The Boss stiffened. He took this thing personally.

'. . . now that I know he is here in this great town with a large sum of money in his pocket, I can't help being in mortal fear for him.'

The Boss mottled. What a thing for the Pierrots to be saying about the town that had made them welcome! He didn't know what the sketch was, but it'd be out to-morrow.

The Boss opened his programme and struck a match.

By God, it was Ibsen!

By ten o'clock Hoy Haven was a blaring, blazing, spinning, screaming gallimaufry of hilarity. Holidaymakers who could not embark at once on the pleasure of their chosen torture, stood in queues to wait their turn, blared at by every type of brassy sound yet invented, chugged at by steam engines, gas engines, Diesel engines, petrol engines, and every sort of engine capable of making the ground shudder; flickered over by revolving lights of every colour, sucking toffee apples, licking iced cornets, guzzling peanuts, and gazing with anticipation at the flung-about and screaming bodies where, in due course, they would be flung about, screaming, themselves.

To-morrow, next week, or whenever their holiday was over, it was back to pinch and scrape and the shadow of a rainy day. But this was their moment, a grubby, sweaty, raucous moment, utterly painful, utterly carefree, held in timelessness by ring after ring of lights. Outside were atom bombs. Here was camaraderie.

Through the camaraderie strode the Boss, his bowler hat jammed over his ears, quite alone, and seeing how low the bowler was nobody spoke to it. When the Boss had his bowler jammed over his ears, you kept a civil tongue in your head or preferably none, and edged as far away as you could.

'Ibsen!' said the Boss forcibly to the poster of the Bearded Lady. 'What is Hoy coming to?' he demanded of the

Fortune Teller's booth, while Gipsy Rosa shrank further into it. 'On my Pier,' he marvelled at the Whip. 'Ibsen!' he scowled at the switchback train, screaming past him. 'Six shillings,' he said to the swings. 'Six shillings for nothing.' 'Six shillings for what?' he put it to the Chinese Laundry. 'Damned, insulting, rubbishy nothing!' he hurled at the Houp-la.

'It's an outrage and I won't stand for it,' he informed a stall-holder, who paled and hurriedly replaced a horrible ash-tray with a horrible Present from Hoy.

His favourite pier without a pierrot! Ibsen! Who let him on? he'd have a word with Joe to-morrow. Getting careless, that's what Bagwash was. He'd have a word with that other Joe too.

Merrivale indeed!

'Going up, Boss?' said the Corsican Bandit outside the Leaning Tower ingratiatingly. He was new and hadn't heard about the bowler hat.

'Shut up, you,' said the Boss. He plonked down a shilling.

And presently there he stood, Master Builder that he was, swaying above the pleasure city he had built and finding it good and bright and happy and wholesome. And value for money. There he stood at the top of his swaying tower and the giggling couples around him looked at him and giggled a bit more.

Slowly the Boss eased his bowler hat and raised it an inch.

It was better up here.

Tuesday morning is to any Repertory Company what Monday morning is to everyone else. The sun may be shining or the fog may have blotted everything out, it makes no difference. If you are playing in weekly Rep. Tuesday morning is as flat as a pancake. You will be spending it sitting in a huddled circle on a partially lit stage surrounded by the first act of last night's play, feeling washed-out by last night's emotions, part triumph and mainly terror, resulting in practically no sleep at all, and not yet kindled by the vista of new excitements and terrors which you are certain to undergo when the curtain rises on the new play next week.

The Last of Mrs. Cheyney. Arms and the Man. The Second Mrs. Tanqueray. French without Tears. Whatever the play you did last week, it will be the first read-through of whatever play you are doing next week, by Shaw, by Pinero, by Coward, by Priestley, or, very rarely, by some ambitious author in the company.

Peter Merrivale was on the second act of his own. If he found time to finish it, which at his present rate of endeavour and progress seemed doubtful, he would put it on here and invite every management in London and Spotlight to come down and see it. Bill Bluebird would be certain to come.

To-day was Tuesday, and all unconscious of Nemesis in a jammed-down bowler hat imminently bearing down on them and already arrived at the Red Mill, the site of which had as usual put it in a worse temper than before, the company were having their first reading of this week's Importance. By Oscar Wilde.

They sat in a circle, uttering at one another with one seat empty which Rose la Fleur, the heavy, had so far failed to fill. Peter Merrivale was uttering for her. He sat facing his company, his book spread on the table in front of him, surrounded by loose sheets of paper on all of which he scribbled furiously, jotting down producer's notes as they occurred to him. It wasn't easy to improve on a Gielgud production with, let's face it, an inferior cast, but that was no reason for not trying to. This time he'd get the Merrivale touch into the thing or die in the attempt. Maybe Bill Bluebird would stay over to see it. Thank God he hadn't seen Hedda. What a performance! He glared at Antony Crispin.

'The army lists of the last forty years are here,' said Tony with great clarity. 'These delightful records,' he announced, 'should have been my constant study. (Rushes to bookcase and tears books out),' he mumbled quickly to himself. 'Generals,' he declaimed. 'Mallom. Maxholm Magley,' he recited. A look of anguish crossed his face. 'What awful names they have,' he said sorrowfully.

'Stop,' said Peter Merrivale. He closed his book with public patience. 'That's not the way John Gielgud said it.'

'I know,' said Antony Crispin with equal patience. 'I've always thought John went wrong there.'

'Oh, did you?' said Peter Merrivale. He digested this. 'Well, that's a point of view.'

'I'll get a laugh my way,' said Antony Crispin.

'Not in Hoy you won't,' said Wilfrid Wilbraham.

'Oh to hell with Hoy,' said Peter Merrivale.

'And to hell with you, Joe,' said a voice from the doorway. It emerged, strong and heartfelt, from beneath a jammed-down bowler hat. Having expressed itself, it moved relentlessly down the empty aisle towards the stage.

'I want a word with you, Joe,' it announced, having got there. Peter Merrivale recognized the six-shilling stall, who had left scowling after the first act. Awful thought! Had he come for his money back?

'Sorry,' he said. 'This is private.'

'Is it now?' said the Boss. He walked firmly up the four steps that in happier years had led so many youngsters on to the stage to help the comedian out with the chorus and collect a prize earned, in the main, by their clapping relations. 'Is it now,' he repeated, and ran his eyes over the slightly surprised but prepared-to-be-amused circle of young faces. He'd give them something to laugh at.

'Are you the Boss of this show here,' he asked the Boy with the Beard.

'Well, yes,' said Peter Merrivale. 'I suppose I am.'

'Well,' said the Boss, 'I'm the Boss of Hoy Haven.'

He waited for the effect. Nothing happened. Just for a moment the Boss missed his fairground where everybody trembled at sight. Then he clamped down his bowler hat a bit more and spoke straight to the point.

'I've come to clear you out,' he said, 'and you'll do me a favour if you go quiet.'

This time he got his effect. There was quite a silence.

'You mean,' said the Boy with the Beard, 'you want us to go?'

'That's it, Joe,' said the Boss, 'and the sooner the better.'

'But why,' asked a chit in trousers—a girl chit. 'What have we done?'

'We've paid our rent,' said a lad with wavy hair.

'In advance,' said the Boy with the Beard.

The chit detached herself from the group, came forward, and stuck her receding chin level with his.

'What have you got against us?' she demanded.

The Boss stuck his chin back at her.

'You're not pierrots,' he accused them.

They didn't get it.

'Well, that's no crime,' said a young shaver with the nerve to giggle.

The Boss withered him.

'That's where you're wrong, Joe,' he said. 'This is Hoy Haven Pier.'

'Well?' said the chit. She made it sound like 'so what.'

'Hoy Haven Pier,' said the Boss, 'has Pierrots. It has had the Pierrots every year since I built it. Mind you,' he admitted fairly, 'some years they've been better than others, but,' he thumped the producer's table, 'but, every year on Hoy Haven Pier there's Pierrots.'

'Well, there aren't any this year,' said the Boy with the Beard.

'And what are you going to do about it,' said the chinning chit.

The Boss looked at those steady grey eyes with instinctive approval. He knew a fighter when he saw one and he liked fighters even when he didn't like what they were fighting for.

'Now take it easy, lass,' he said, 'you're going off my pier, and if you're sensible you'll go off quiet, and if you're not sensible you'll go, anyway.'

Peter Merrivale remembered he was a business man.

'I've got a contract,' he said. He sounded like a defiant little boy.

'You got it when I wasn't looking,' said the Boss. He

sounded like another little boy. 'The fellow that gave it to you would be out on his ear if he hadn't been with me thirty years. I've had a word with him this morning,' he said with a certain grim satisfaction.

'A contract is a contract,' said the Chit as one voicing the creed of her Fathers,' and you know that as well as anyone.'

'That's right,' said the Boss mildly.

'You may be the Boss of Hoy Haven,' said the Chit, 'but you can be sued the same as anyone else.'

'Hark at our Tass,' said one young shaver to another young shaver.

'Who do you think you are,' demanded the Chit carried away. 'God?'

'Round these parts,' said the Boss.

Peter Merrivale felt it was time to come to his stage-manager's aid. 'That's what you think,' he said bravely. 'But we've leased this theatre, and we've got a contract to prove it, and right now you're trespassing on private property and,' he added the crushing blow, 'holding up a rehearsal.'

The Boss looked at the quivering beard.

'See here, sonny,' he said, 'I got nothing against you personally, but you've got to go. You're not right for Hoy.'

'And what do you expect us to do,' said the high and mighty Chit, back to battle. 'Close down the theatre? Break up our season? Ruin our careers? I'll have you know,' she informed him, 'that Bill Bluebird has promised to come down and see us.'

'Who?' said the Boss.

'Oh, what's the use?' said the Lad with wavy hair to the ceiling.

'Do you realize how much money we've sunk in this?'

demanded the Boy with the Beard. He stopped back and timed it. 'One hundred pounds.' He made it sound enormous. 'Are you prepared to make good the loss.'

'Yes,' said the Boss cheerfully. He sat down. He eased up his bowler hat. He nearly smiled.

'Now look here,' he said, 'I'm a reasonable man. . . .'

'Oh, don't be childish,' said the Chit crossly. She turned her back on him.

'I'm a reasonable man,' repeated the Boss unmoved, 'and I'm willing to pay for my mistakes. Not that it was my mistake, mind you, but I'm responsible,' He looked a little sad. 'Yes,' he repeated, 'I'm responsible. But that doesn't alter facts. You're not right for Hoy, so you've got to go.'

The company was silent. The old boy sounded as though he meant it. 'But you've been put to some expense and it's only right that you shouldn't lose. So I'll give you a hundred pounds, that's your whole capital, son, and you're lucky to see it back—I started on twenty—and another fifty pounds over for your trouble, and that's more than you'd make if you stayed here all season.' He waited.

'He's got something,' said the Boy with the Beard, stroking it.

The Boss beamed at him. 'What's more,' he said, a wave of unusual generosity sweeping over him, 'I'll give you your tickets back to town. What d'you say?' He waited.

'First class?' asked the young shaver with the nerve to giggle.

'*You'll* walk,' said the Boss savagely. He waited. 'Well,' he said.

The company looked at one another. They were waiting for a lead. And loyally restraining themselves from doing mental arithmetic while they waited. Tassel Trevillion gave it to them. She picked up his umbrella and handed it to him.

'Here's your brolly,' she said. 'Good morning. And you can take your thirty pieces of silver with you.'

The Boss mottled. He jammed down the bowler. 'So that's your answer, is it?' he asked.

'Yes,' said the Chit.

The Boy with the Beard hesitated. The Chit took time off to glare at him.

'Definitely,' said the Boy with the Beard.

All the young shavers nodded wisely and the fat old lady who had just come in and couldn't have known what it was all about nodded too.

'That's our answer,' she said confidently, 'and now you know.' She took out her vanity case and powdered her nose. Trouble with the landlord was routine to Rose la Fleur.

'In that case,' said the Boss, 'the offer's off. I'll close you down and I'll drive you out.'

'You can't do it,' said the Boy with the Beard.

'Can't I?' said the Boss with as much give as granite. 'You'll see.' He jammed his bowler hat over his ears and started to stomp out.

'And that,' said Rose la Fleur, an Edith Evans condescending to the ceiling, 'is what we get for bringing Hedda to Hoy.'

Every word could be heard in the gallery—had there been one. The figure nearing the exit caught them with ease. It turned.

'To hell with Hedda,' it shouted back.

The Peter Merrivale Repertory Players took five minutes off, agreed that the old Josser couldn't do anything much—who did he think he was? Howard and Wyndham?—and went back to their rehearsal. The old Josser went back to his office and sulked. Who did they think they were? Sarah Bernhardt?

They'd lose their capital now, young fools! That chit. She'd put them up to it. They'd have done as he asked but for her. Well, she'd be coming to him yet, with tears in her eyes, begging for her ticket back to town. And when she'd begged enough he'd give it to her, just to be rid of her, rid of the lot of them, and have his pierrots back on his favourite pier.

To Hell with Hedda. He'd told them straight, hadn't he?

Having sulked for half an hour, the Boss took stock. He realized with a shock that carrying out his threat was going to cost him money. He faced it and accepted it. You always had to pay for your mistakes and his mistake had been to grow old and let other people take over things he should have kept in his own hands.

'I'll close you down and I'll drive you out,' he'd promised. Now what was the cheapest way of doing it?

[iv]

All that week the weather was as bright as a gypsy's future, but it was still early in the season and Hoy was not as full as it was going to be. You could book a room at Hoy Hotel by walking in and asking for it. There was no queue outside the Louis Quinze Grill. Business at the Aquarium

was only so-so. The Red Mill might just as well have been
white tiles and nobody went into the Palace of Art—but
that was only to be expected.

Yet the theatres were packed out and the piers were
doing nicely—all three of them.

On the surface, the Boss' favourite pier appeared much as
usual. Holiday-makers strolled about, eating whelks, eating
hokey-pokey, patronizing the Camera Obscura, listening to
the concerts and having fun, while a few, a very few,
strolled further on and drifted into Hedda Gabler and came
out muttering. But under the surface the Boss was getting
to work and the first intimation of it arrived on Saturday
morning with the usual last-minute rush to borrow the
props for next Monday's opening.

'Yes,' said Rose la Fleur, 'these will do nicely.'

She picked up a pair of lorgnettes from the pile of
Victoriana spread on the counter and looked through them
with approval at the rest.

'A handbag!' she boomed unaccountably. She reached
for Lady Windemere's fan and fanned herself.

'That,' said the very young owner of the Old Curiositie
Shoppe, 'will be . . . Thirteen . . . Fifteen five . . . Twenty-
two pounds, two and ninepence.'

Rose la Fleur eyed him. So might Mrs. Siddons have
looked at an indelicate suggester.

'I beg your pardon,' she said.

'Cash,' said the Very Young Owner.

Rose la Fleur gave a patient sigh. (The Silver Chord.)
She put down Lady Windemere's Fan. She sat down. She
prepared to be sweet and reasonable. But, just in case, she
retained the lorgnettes.

'Mr.—ah—Curiositie Shoppe,' she said. 'You are no doubt confused. We are the Merrivale Repertory Players. We have—ah—an Arrangement.'

'No more borrowing,' said the Young Man. 'Orders,' he explained. 'Sorry, old girl,' he condescended.

Up went the lorgnettes.

'Old girl!' boomed Lady Bracknell.

'Sorry, ma,' said the Young Man. 'It's the Boss' orders.'

Jocasta failed to quail.

'Don't know what you've done to rile him,' said the Young Man, 'but he's riled all right. No more Arrangements—No more Credit. I'd like to oblige you, Lady, but . . .'

Cleopatra turned the Old Nile on him.

'Do it for the theatre,' she vibrated. 'Do it for me,' she pulsated.

'Sorry, ma,' said the Young Owner. 'It's more than my site's worth.'

'Is this final?' asked Mrs. Tanqueray.

'Guess so,' said the Young Owner cheerfully.

Mrs. Siddons stood up. (Rôles were running out.)

'In that case,' she announced, 'I shall take my custom to your competitors.'

'That's right ma,' said the Young Owner with a grin. 'You take it to them.'

Control snapped.

'Oh, teach your grandmother to suck eggs,' said Rose la Fleur.

She swept out.

Anyway, she consoled herself in the street, I've got away with the lorgnettes.

Lunch was a gobbled sandwich and a dwelt-over beer. The Merrivale Players took it in the public bar of the Lobster Smack, where, freed from the scum of trippers, they could concentrate on their own affairs and throw an idle dart, unmolested by the frequenting fishermen, who had long since abandoned their early attempts to point out that it was a nice day for a sail.

'Would you believe it,' said Rose la Fleur to a wan little wisp, who would certainly play Ophelia if they ever got round to putting on Hamlet, 'he refused. Refused! Never in all my twenty-five years' experience,' she underestimated, 'has such a thing happened to me. I tell you, Marilyn, you could have knocked me down with a feather.'

'Same again, darling,' said the Wisp to the barmaid. 'Never mind, Rose,' she consoled, 'we'll get our props some way.'

'Oh, we'll get them all right,' said Rose la Fleur, 'I'm not worrying about that. It isn't the props, it's the principle. When Trade refuses to co-operate with the Theatre, Trade's in a bad way.'

'And so's the Theatre, darling,' said the Wisp. She drained her tankard.

Tassel Trevillion came in. She looked livid.

'A pint,' she threw at the barmaid. 'What's in those sandwiches?'

'Galantine,' said the barmaid.

'Oh God,' said Tass. She took her pint over to the bench. She donked it on the wooden table.

'Would you believe it,' she said. 'They wanted me to buy it.'

The others were with her in a flash.

'Not the garden set,' they said in horror.

'Every stick of furniture we need for the Importance,' said Tass. 'I thought Peter was exaggerating, so I went down to Caffin, Son and Nephew, myself. I saw the nephew,' she frowned. 'Boss' orders indeed,' she fumed. 'You'd think the man owned the town.'

'He does,' said the Wisp. She drained her tankard. 'If you ask me, I think we've had it, darling.'

'Had it!' boomed Boadicea. 'Child, child, you don't know what you're saying. Credit can help the Theatre, but No Credit can't close it down.'

'We'll find a way,' said Tass. 'We'll pinch the deck chairs off the pier if we must.'

'That's an idea,' said Rose la Fleur. 'There's a very nice ticket collector there. Married.' She shook her head.

'My landlady's got a gorgeous aspidistra,' said the Wisp. I'm sure she'd lend it to us.'

'The trouble,' mused Tass, 'is going to be top hats.'

'Does the Boss own the undertakers?' asked the Wisp.

'Bound to,' said Rose la Fleur. 'Blasted monopolist.'

Tass brooded.

'Wish I'd voted Labour. No I don't,' she corrected herself.

'Something ought to be done about the Boss,' said the Wisp thoughtfully. She pulled out her lipstick.

'Not that way,' said Tass at once. 'But I agree with you. Something should be done. I wish this was Chicago,' she sighed.

Antony Crispin and Wilfrid Wilbraham came in.

'No morning coats,' said Tony.

'And we can't collect the cleaning without cash,' said Wilfrid. He hurled a savage dart and scored a double twenty. 'See that,' he said, surprised.

Peter Merrivale came storming in.

'Here's a nice state of affairs,' he told them. 'They won't print our programmes.'

'Who cares?' said Tass. 'We'll chalk it on a black-board.'

'The Boss owns the chalk,' said Wilfrid.

'Does he?' said the Wisp impressed.

'What I really want to know,' said Antony Crispin, 'is what the Boss thinks he's playing at.'

'He wants to close us down, darling,' said the Wisp, 'hadn't you gathered?'

'Well, he can't do it this way,' said Peter Merrivale. His beard stuck out.

'You bet he can't,' said Tass. She drained her beer and rose with great determination. 'What's more,' she announced, 'I'm off to tell him so.'

For the first time that season she put her arms into the sleeves of her camel-hair.

Clearly it was once more unto the breach.

Past the Aquarium. Past the Palace of Art—what a monstrosity! Through the Victory Arcade—oh God! Past the Red Mill—a Windmill on top of a W.C.—a Con-venience turned into a Carnival. . . . There you had the whole of the blasted town. And there you had the whole of the blasted owner, blast him.

Tass was being unfair to the Boss. How should she know of the frequent frowns and mutters of 'They shouldn't have put it there.'

Past the Hokey-Pokey Parlour, past the picture postcards, past the sugar beards—couldn't get away from them any-where, past some horrible shops—who cared what they were called? And so to the headquarters of that unspeakable man.

The offices of Hoy Haven Development and Enterprises, Ltd., were situated opposite the Railway Station. The Boss had picked the site sixty years ago, even before the railway extension ever got there, and it always gave him great pleasure to think that in the end the railway had come to him instead of he to the railway. In these sixty years the Hoy Haven Development and Enterprises, Ltd., had enterprised and developed all over the place, but their office hadn't changed at all.

'Good solid furniture,' the Boss had said to his wife on the day he bought it.

'Yes, dear,' his wife had said.

'The Name of the Firm in Gold Letters on the window to show we're no fly-by-nights.'

'Yes, dear.'

'A nice Turkey carpet to give a bit of colour on a cold day.'

'Yes, dear.'

And this time she must have been listening, for she followed it with a demand for a new drawing-room carpet, as though they could afford it yet. 'You shall have your carpet,' he had promised, 'but you'll have to wait for it.' And in three years he'd given it to her and a fur coat too. Not as good as the one he gave her later, mind you.

The Boss was sitting at his solid mahogany desk, being gesticulated at by a pleading figure when Tass stormed in.

'You bloodsucker,' she said. 'You dictator! You obstinate silly old man. God, I wish I could tell you what I think of you.'

The Boss took in the angry face. A certain softening, that

in the Boss might be called a smile, touched his hewn features.

'Sit down, lass,' he said. 'I'll attend to you in a minute. You were saying, Joe?'

'I was saying you can't do this to me, Boss,' said the gesticulating figure. Tass recognized the whelkman from the foot of the pier. 'I'm paying my rent, aren't I? I'm making you a fortune, aren't I? Four pound fifteen you took off me last week, didn't you? You can't do it, I tell you. You can't close me down.'

'You can't, you know,' said Tass from nowhere.

'I'm not closing you down, Joe,' said the Boss patiently. 'I'm transferring you to a better pitch, if you'd only realize it.'

'I'm happy where I am,' said the whelkman stubbornly. 'Everyone knows me and everyone likes me, and I'm making a fortune. You ought to see the people that say good evening to me even when they don't buy,' he boasted. 'And good evening to-day means a saucer to-morrow. It's building up lovely. By the end of the season I'll be a little gold mine, see if I ain't.'

'You'll have to go dig yourself elsewhere, Joe,' said the Boss.

'And what about my goodwill?' demanded the whelk-man. 'What about my customers?'

'You won't have many customers, Joe,' said the Boss. 'Not when I've closed the Obscura, and the Fun Parlour, and taken away the Band. There won't be much custom left, Joe, when I've done what I mean to do to the pier.'

The whelkman looked astonished. 'It sounds like you're closing it down, Boss.'

'Very nearly,' said the Boss. He shot a look at Tass. She'd

got it all right. 'That's what I'm telling you. I know it's hard, Joe,' he conceded, 'but you won't be the loser. I've got a nice little pitch for you next to the Houp-la.'

'Don't want it,' said the whelkman sulkily. 'Spend all my profits on them blasted rings.' He gazed through—

Hoy Development and Enterprises

—in gold letters on the window into a gambler's ruined fortune.

'Let me stay, boss. I'll make a fortune for you,' he went back to wheedling.

The Boss considered. After all, a whelk stall, one way or another, wouldn't affect the issue.

'Have it your own way, Joe,' he said. 'Stay where you are. But it's my belief you'll be back here next month begging me for another pitch.'

'Thank you, Boss,' said the whelkman, transfigured. He darted for his hat. He made for the door. 'You won't regret it,' he promised. 'I'll make a fortune for you.'

The door closed with a jubilant slam.

The Boss turned to the Chit. She was looking at him with her lips as thin as she could make them.

'I get it,' she said. 'You're closing down the pier to get rid of us.'

'That's right,' said the Boss.

'And you've shut down on our credit and nobody in the town dares to help us.'

'Thought they wouldn't,' said the Boss with satisfaction.

'You're nothing but a blackmailer,' said Tass. 'Nobody can breathe in this town without your permission.'

'That's right,' said the Boss.

'I despise you,' said Tass.

'That's right,' said the Boss. 'What's more, I like you for it.'

Tass akimboed. 'Oh, you do,' she said.

'But that doesn't mean I'm going to let you stay on my pier,' went on the Boss. 'I don't want you in Hoy, and I'm going to get you out of Hoy and the sooner you make up your minds to it the better for all of us.'

Tass sniffed.

'Look, lass,' said the Boss. 'I made you an offer and you turned it down. I'll make you another. I'll give you seventy-five pounds and I'll pay your fares back to London—third class,' he made it quite clear, 'and if you're sensible, you'll ring up that young Joe with the beard and bring him here to clinch it. There's the 'phone.' He pointed.

Tass folded her arms. 'We're staying,' she announced.

The Boss folded his. 'You're going.'

'We're staying,' said Tass leaning forward at him, 'if it takes every penny we've got.'

'You're going,' roared the Boss, 'and it won't take every penny I've got—not by a long chalk.'

'It'll cost you more than it'll cost us,' said Tass, talking turkey.

This sobered the Boss. 'Do you think I don't know that,' he said bitterly. 'Do you think I like mucking about with my favourite pier just because a lot of stubborn young idiots will play their piffle on it? Do you think I like telling a lot of honest hard-working people to uproot their trade and get a living elsewhere? Do you think I like the idea of all the people who'd go on my pier going on to that upstart pier that got built when I wasn't looking? Do you think I like all that, you Chit?' He thumped the solid mahogany desk. It was just as well it was solid.

'Then why are you doing it?' demanded the Chit.

'Because you're not right for Hoy,' roared the Boss. 'Because Hoy's my town, and what's not right for Hoy has got to go, even, even if it's my own flesh and blood.'

Tass looked at him.

'Yes,' she said, 'that's just what you would do. You'd drive away your own flesh and blood if you thought they weren't right for your blasted town.'

'That's right,' said the Boss. But his wrath had left him and he sat very still. 'I sent my boy away because he wouldn't see eye to eye with me about Hoy. And I've never seen him since. And,' he looked her straight in the face, 'I've never regretted it. So you see, lass,' he finished soberly, 'you haven't got a chance.'

A tinge of compassion crept into Tass' anger. Only a tinge.

'Why must old men be so stubborn?' she asked. 'My grandfather drove my father out. I've never discovered why, and I've never discovered from where. And father changed his name and they've never seen each other since. And father says he's never regretted it—and he's a liar just like you are.'

'Is he?' said the Boss. 'I daresay he is. But I daresay your grandfather was right to do as he did—just as I was.'

'And I daresay you were both idiots,' said Tass. 'But at least Dad's got Mum and me and his friends. What have you got?' she challenged.

'I've got Hoy Haven,' said the Boss.

'You can have it,' said Tass.

'Thanks,' said the Boss gravely, 'I will. I'm eighty-one years old, and it'll last my time. I'm not saying I don't miss my wife, lass, but I couldn't stay the hand of nature, could I? I couldn't stop Martha dying, could I? Forty years, and never a cross word. If your Dad's as happy with his wife as I was with mine, he's got nothing to grumble about.'

'But was she happy?' asked Tass.

'Eh?' said the Boss startled.

'I bet,' said Tass, 'that all she ever said was "Yes dear." '

The Boss considered. 'That's right,' he said. 'I guess she found it easy. Sometimes it crossed my mind,' again the shadow of a smile touched his face, 'that she wasn't always listening.'

'I bet she wasn't,' said Tass. She grinned. 'Just as I never listen to Mum.'

'Well, you'll listen to me, my girl.' The Boss went back to business. 'You get your company out of here. If you'd like a little holiday yourself,' he offered, 'I'll see if I can't fix you up with something to bring in the pennies.'

'You've only got to say the word, eh?' said Tass.

'That's right,' said the Boss, not getting it.

'Well, don't bother,' said Tass. 'I've got into the theatre and I'm staying in the theatre. I've had to fight it out with my father, and I'm damned if I'm going to fight it out with you.'

'What did your Dad want you to do?' asked the Boss interested.

Tass sniffed. 'He wanted me to be a doctor. Five years—to learn to keep people like you alive. What for?'

'My son wanted to be a doctor,' said the Boss. 'Don't believe in doctors.' He looked at Hoy Enterprises spelt backwards. He remembered he had said this to his wife the day the doctors had told him there was no hope. 'Yes, dear,' his wife had said. Next morning she was dead.

'You don't believe in anything,' said Tass.

'I believe in Hoy,' said the Boss, 'and I believe in getting you out of Hoy. Now be a good little lass and go,' he coaxed. 'You're giving us a lot of trouble.'

'We'll give you a lot more trouble before we're through,' said Tass. 'Now be a dear,' she coaxed, 'and lay off. After all, what harm do we do you?'

'You're not right for Hoy,' said the Boss doggedly.

A stubborn chit glared. A stubborn old man glared back.

"Oh, to Hell with Hoy,' roared the grandchild, 'and to hell with you.'

She burst into tears and ran out of the room.

The Boss looked after her. Unaccountably, he felt a little lonely. But he pulled himself together.

'And to Hell with Hedda,' roared the Grandad.

[v]

On Monday night in the concert hall at the end of the Boss' favourite pier the curtain went up on The Importance. Never mind how. It did. What's more, it was only seven minutes late.

The audience consisted mainly of landladies, there to view their own furniture.

On the whole the play went well. The audience seemed to grasp rather more of it than they had of Hedda. There was quite a scream in the third act when Jack Worthing, enthusiastically pulling out the books, knocked over the bookcase. It came from the landlady who had lent it. Next morning she took it back.

The gratified company did not bother to take its make-up off before setting out for home. Art for Arts' sake every time, of course, but a little applause was nice as well, and this was the warmest they had heard at Hoy. It couldn't be called bringing the house down, as Wilfrid Wilbraham did not fail to point out, but it was a big improvement on the puzzled silences that had greeted Hedda's suicide. Or the frantic scuffle for the exits following on The Father.

'With any luck,' said Antony Crispin, optimist, 'they'll tell their friends.'

'And with any luck,' said Wilfrid Wilbraham, 'they won't ask for free seats.'

'I signed an autograph,' swanked the Wisp.

They straggled down the twinkling pier.

'Not so many people as usual to-night,' observed Peter Merrivale.

'The Fun Fair's closed,' said Tass.

'Blast him,' said Peter. He looked sadly at the coloured lights that outlined the pleasure contours of the pier. They wandered on past the shuttered windows of the sideshows, mourning each separate booth where before they used to curse it roundly. They arrived at the foot of the pier.

The shooting gallery was closed. So was the skating rink. The sugar beards had fluffed away. The Camera Obscura had flown. The fortune-teller had funked it.

But one interior flung out a defiant naphtha.

'Whelks, darling?' asked Tass.

'But of course,' said Peter.

The palookas from the Pavilion gathered round the booth, their make-up all the more garish for the naphtha, a faithful little knot supporting their only supporter. A few yards away the Pleasure Beach glared and blared and greedily sucked up the pennies poured into it. But here it was quiet save for the lapping of the waves.

'Another saucer, Miss?' asked the whelkman.

'Sure,' said Tass gallantly.

You had to support a supporter, hadn't you?

By Saturday the Palookas at the Pavilion were fifteen pounds down on the week, and that in spite of a providential rainstorm that had driven thirty-seven people into a matinee. This drop would not have depressed Bill Bluebird unduly had it happened to one of his £10,000 productions, though he would no doubt have enquired into the reasons for it, spoken to somebody heatedly, but with charm, and hurriedly shovelled a part of the backing on to one of his buddies. But to the Peter Merrivale Players, already working at a loss, it could only spell one thing. Equity minimums and a share of the profits. And it seemed unlikely that there were going to be many profits on Houpla—We Live, due to be played next week with black curtains and no furniture. Expressionism: an Avant Garde hangover which had clearly been invented to solve their particular problem, as Wilfrid Wilbraham pointed out.

Fifteen pounds to the bad. Tass faced this unwelcome fact together with the now unwelcome plate of whelks.

'Business has been looking up to-day, Miss,' said the whelkman, almost himself again. 'Mark my words,' he said, 'we've got a little gold mine here.'

'It's Saturday,' said Wilfrid Wilbraham realistically.

The whelkman's face fell. But he tugged it up again.

'It's a good sign,' he maintained obstinately.

Fifteen pounds. How long could they last out? Three weeks? A month? And the Boss telling her he told her so. Tass pushed away her saucer of whelks and made off.

'There goes Tass in one of her mists,' said Antony Crispin.

'Let her be,' said Peter Merrivale wisely.

'Fat-headed old dodderer!' Like an absentminded moth Tass had made for the lights and was now mumbling to herself amid the glare and blare of Pleasure Beach. 'Obstinate old kill-joy,' she said staring straight at a screaming Giant Wheel. 'Was there anything to be said for his point of view?' she asked the snake-coiled painting of the charmer. 'Not a thing,' she agreed with the giraffe nodding out of Noah's Ark. 'He won't be happy till he makes everybody as miserable as he is himself,' she informed the searchlights, playing silver and green and crimson over her upturned angry face.

Why did she rather like him? There was nothing to like about him. Hard, mean, obstinate. 'I hate him,' she told the revolving roundabout.

Maybe he was like that because he was unhappy. Well, whose fault was that? Tass threw a vague ring in the direction of A Present from Hoy. Doddering old fathead!

'That's not the way, lass,' said a voice behind her.

It was the doddering old fathead.

'That's not the way to throw at Houp-la,' he said. 'Here, I'll show you. Four rings.' He plonked down threepence.

The stall-holder handed them up sadly.

'Now what shall we make for?' asked the Boss. He ran a calculating eye over the display.

'That watch,' said Tass.

'Too greedy,' said the Boss. The stall-holder relaxed. 'We'll try for A Present From Hoy.'

He flung. The ring hovered, hardly hesitated, and settled over the block with the china shoe.

'There you are, lass,' he said smugly, as the resigned stall-holder passed it up. 'A Present from Hoy.'

The coloured searchlights played over their faces.

'Pretty, isn't it?' said the Boss. He handed her the horror.

'Are you giving it to me?' asked Tass dangerously.

'That's right,' said the Boss. 'I've got three more rings, haven't I?'

The stall-holder shivered.

'It must be a long time since you're given anyone anything,' said Tass.

The Boss considered.

'That's right,' he said. Perhaps he had forgotten his large subscription to the Lifeboats and to every charity in town. Perhaps he had forgotten the free annual outings to Pleasure Beach for the Orphanage, Sailors' Widows and Children, Disabled ex-Service men, and one year—an experiment never repeated—Expectant Mothers.

The coloured searchlights played over them again. They came from the Tower of Pisa.

'Like to come up lass?' asked the Boss. 'It's pretty up there. On me,' he assured her.

Tass looked at the swaying Tower.

She grinned. Maybe she'd get a chance to push him off.

Swaying unprecariously above the lights of Hoy, Tass stood on the top of Pisa and looked down.

'It's beautiful from here,' she said fairmindedly.

'It is that,' agreed the Boss. 'Hoy's a beauty, however you look at her.' He stretched out a generous arm to embrace town, hills, sea and all. 'It didn't look like this when I first took over.'

'I bet it didn't,' said Tass.

'Just a village,' said the Boss, 'and a handful of fishing smacks. And if anybody wanted to spend the day here they had to bring their own lunch—till I started catering.'

'Cup of tea twopence?' said Tass.

'A penny,' said the Boss. 'You try charging twopence for a cup of tea in eighteen-ninety and see what they'd say to you then. What's more, we did a lunch for tenpence later on. Joint, two veg., and a darn sight better than you pay five bob for at the Louis Quinze to-day. Not that the Louis Quinze isn't value for money as things are at present, but you could taste what you were eating at our place. The Missus cooked and I passed the plates up. And we did the washing-up together till we could afford a lassie to do it for us. Ten bob a week—and her lunch,' he remembered. 'It seemed an awful lot of money then. But that was nothing to what we paid her later on when we left her to run the place. Do you know,' he turned to Tass, 'there were times when that lass made seven quid a week! But pay a good man well and he won't rob you, that's what I always say.'

'That's what my father says,' said Tass.

'And he's right,' said the Boss. 'Reckon I'd like your father. Pity you don't take after him.' he added with an unexpected twinkle.

'Oh, but I do,' said Tass, 'Mother says I'm the very chip of him.'

'Does she?' said the Very Old Block.

'Just as obstinate,' explained the Chip.

'My boy was obstinate too,' said the Block.

'And I suppose you're not,' said the Chip.

'I know what I want,' said the Block, 'if you call that obstinate—all right!'

The Chip leaned over the parapet. She took in Hoy.

'And this is what you want.'

'That's right,' said the Block. 'Isn't she a beauty?'

'From up here,' said the Chip. 'It's only when you get

down that you realize that it's sweaty and noisy and dirty and,' her lip curled, 'cheap.'

'That's right,' said the Block. 'Value for money.'

'Money!' said the Chip. 'It's no use, we don't speak the same language.'

'Oh yes we do,' said the Block. 'Only we speak it differently, that's all.'

'Oh no we don't,' said the Chip. 'Money's the only word that means anything to you.'

A hooter went off. As if by magic the piers went out. The coloured searchlights wiped themselves away. The crowd began to mill in one direction. Odd lights about the fairground blinked out one by one. . . .

'Another day over,' said the Block. 'Time for bed, lass. Coming down?'

'Let the others go first,' said the Chip. 'It's nice up here.'

The Chip and the Old Block leaned over the parapet together and watched Hoy Haven going home.

'You know,' said the Block, 'you're not being fair to me. You've got it in for me because I'm driving you out of the town.'

'Well?' said the Chip.

'By my standards I've got to do it,' said the Block. 'I aim to make Hoy a tonic and you wouldn't call Hedda a tonic, would you now?'

'You wouldn't understand about Hedda,' said the Chip, 'or anything we stand for.'

'Oh yes I would,' said the Block. 'It's Art.'

'Yes, it is,' said the Chip defiantly.

'I respect Art,' said the Block. 'I've often wished I had time to understand it. Maybe when I retire I'll buy some pictures, and if God spares me to look at them often enough maybe I'll understand what the fellows are driving at. I respect Art,' the Block repeated. 'But Hoy Haven isn't the place for it.'

'You're right there,' said the Chip, thinking of their audiences, 'but that's all the more reason to try and educate it.'

'No,' said the Block with great violence.

The startled Chip jumped.

'No,' said the Block, 'Hoy isn't a school. Hoy's a holiday for people who work hard all the year round and want to enjoy themselves. They don't want to be bothered with Art. We've got a Palace of Art, and it's the only side-show that runs at a loss.'

'People ought to want to bother,' said the Chip weakly.

'You've got to take people as they come,' said the Block into the darkness. 'Maybe it's all wrong that they prefer George Formby to . . . to . . . Sarah Bernhardt,' he found, 'but George Formby is what they want, and George is what Hoy is going to give them. When the day comes that they queue up for Sarah—if it does come—Hoy will give them Sarah.'

'I still don't see what harm we do,' said the Chip.

'Look,' said the Block. 'I'll make you an offer. I'll give you fifty pounds and your fares back.'

'Don't,' said the Chip, 'not up here.' She ran a hand through her hair. 'Oh dear,' she said. 'I'm tired.' She sat down on a bench.

'Past your bedtime,' said the Block. He sat down beside her. 'Past mine, too,' he admitted.

She leaned against him.

'Come on, lass,' said the Block. 'I'll see you home.'

The Chip stiffened. 'I can see myself home,' she said.

'I'll see you home, lass,' said the Block firmly.

The Chip and the Block glared at one another while the bandit below, waiting to lock up, yawned again.

[vi]

The public didn't take to Houpla—We Live! The takings fell another twelve pounds ten, leaving—well, there's no need to go into that. Final blow, Bill Bluebird, though definitely down with the try-out of his new production 'So This Is Sugar,' failed to come near the pier. And that in spite of practically promising a bumped-into Antony Crispin that he'd be in before the week was out.

The following week was no better. 'Dangerous Corner' more than lived up to its name.

Antony Crispin had taken to getting letters from London and stuffing them without comment into his pocket and being a little uneasy with the company.

'He's going to rat,' said Rose la Fleur. 'I know the signs.'

'Rat!' observed the Wisp.

Wilfrid Wilbraham took to the pubs. Peter Merrivale took to the racing editions in an unsuccessful series of despairing safety bets. But Tass, to fortify her obstinacy, took to the Boss as a weaker spirit takes to drink. She bumped into him on the promenade, she dropped into his office, and once he took her out to lunch. And every time they met they argued, and neither yielded an inch, and a great respect grew up between them and each called the other obstinate.

'Why do you waste your time, Tass?' asked Wilfrid Wilbraham. 'You can't move an ocean or change the face of granite.'

'It does me good to try,' said Tass.

John Gabriel Borkman just about did for the whelkman. They learned this after the show on Saturday night as they gathered round for the now nauseating saucers that were fast becoming their staple nourishment.

'I don't like giving up,' he told them. 'It ought to've been a little gold mine.'

'Where are you going, Joe,' asked Tass. 'Next to the Houp-la?'

'Not me,' said the whelkman. 'I got a nice little pitch by the Victory Arcade. Took me half a morning to talk myself into it.'

'Well,' said Peter Merrivale, 'I wish you luck.'

'Thank you, sir,' said the whelkman. 'Same to you. 'Ere,' he offered, " 'ave another saucer—on the house.'

But Peter had mouched away to the side of the pier and was looking at the pool of light on the black watersilk sea. Tass came over to him. She slipped a rare arm through his.

'Never mind, Peter,' she said. 'I'm sick of whelks, anyway. Let's go on the roundabouts.'

'Can't afford it,' said Peter.

'Come on,' urged Tass. 'Sixpence won't save the day.'

'It never stops at sixpence,' Peter grumbled as she led him off.

And so presently there they were rising and falling on a lion and an ostrich.

'Daisy, Daisy, give me your answer do,' wheezed the steam organ.

'Peter,' shouted Tass coming down, 'let's scrap Mrs. Warren and put on Charley's Aunt.'

'What?' shouted Peter going up. 'For just a moment,' he said as they passed each other, 'I thought you said "Put on Charley's Aunt"!'

'I did,' shouted Tass from the heights.

The roundabout slowed up. The music petered out. Some clambered off; others clambered on.

'Now let me get this clear,' said Peter, staying on his lion. 'You are suggesting that the Merrivale Players should put on Charley's Aunt.' He thrust an impatient shilling at the collector. 'Are you quite crazy?'

'That's right,' said Tass. 'People come to Hoy to enjoy themselves. Well, Charley's Aunt is a damned good farce.'

'And Mrs. Warren is a damned good indictment of society,' said Peter. 'What's more, Rose la Fleur is going to be terrific.'

'What's the point of being terrific if there's no one to see you,' demanded Tass as the music started up again.

'Bill Bluebird might drop in,' shouted Peter from the heights.

'Oh, be your age,' shouted Tass. 'Be older,' she corrected.

'I am my age,' shouted Peter livid. 'If you really want to know, it's not a question of *what* we put on on Monday week, but *if* we put it on.'

They passed each other in silence.

'Broke?' asked Tass next time they came level.

'Busted,' said Peter, the next one.

As the music stopped he prepared to get off. Tass handed the collector a shilling. 'Wait a minute, Peter,' she said. 'How much do you need to put on Charley's Aunt?'

'Salary list and about ten pounds,' said Peter. 'Why?'

The music started. So did the roundabout.

'About eighty pounds,' said Tass. 'All right, Peter, I'll put it up.'

It caught Peter with the lion at its zenith.

'What was that?' he shouted down. 'It sounded as though you said you'd put it up!'

'I did,' shouted Tass.

'You got eighty pounds?'

'Just about,' called Tass. 'For Charley's Aunt,' she said firmly as they met.

'What's the snag,' shouted Peter, being wafted up. 'Want to play the lead?'

'Certainly not,' said Tass. She clouted him as they passed.

'You're crazy,' called Peter. 'With eighty quid we could put on Mrs. Warren.'

'Not with my eighty,' shouted Tass.

They rose and fell while Peter thought the matter over. Charley's Aunt wasn't Mrs. Warren, but it *was* a good farce. A Classic Farce, you could call it. It even had its own kind of poetry. He wouldn't be damning himself for ever by doing it. Think of Charlie Chaplin. Think of Grock. Think of the company breaking up because he couldn't pay them for next week's work.

The roundabout stopped.

'Well?' demanded Tass.

'Well . . .' began Peter.

'Thought I'd find you here,' said Tony Crispin, sudden as a switchback. 'Mind if I join you.' He climbed on to the giraffe.

The collector came round. Tony paid for all three.

'I don't like the look of this,' hissed Tass.

'Rat!' hissed Peter.

It was not until the roundabout was in full motion back home in Tenessee that Tony broached the subject.

'Peter,' he bawled. 'I've had an offer.'

'Bill Bluebird?' bawled Peter.

'No,' bawled Tony. 'Penge!'

'What are you going to do?' bawled Tass grimly.

'What *can* I do?' bawled Tony sheepishly. 'It's London. Practically the West End.'

'Then,' bawled Peter, 'I take it you'll be leaving us next Saturday.'

'Yes,' bawled Tony.

The roundabout stopped. Tony got off looking very red in the face.

'I feel a rat,' he said, 'but . . .'

'Oh, that's all right,' said Peter.

Tony fidgeted a bit, got jostled by two small boys heading simultaneously for the giraffe, refused to arbitrate, and melted away. The collector settled the argument by pushing them both off. It appeared they couldn't pay.

Misfortune brought the small boys together. They stood hand in hand, gazing hungrily at the about-to-rise-and-fall animals.

'What the hell!' said Peter. When you were broke you were broke. He paid for them.

The quarrel started up again. So did the music.

Tass and Peter rose and fell in silence, oblivious of the small boys who were rising and falling not nearly so silently. Tass was thoughtful. Peter moody. As the animals slowed down and the music petered out, he spoke.

'Tass,' he said, 'are you quite sure you want to risk your Rainy Day?'

'Yes,' said Tass.

'Wouldn't it be more sensible to buy a new bonnet and look for a job?'

'Yes,' said Tass.

'After all, you might lose it.'

'Yes,' said Tass.

'All right,' said Peter. 'Have it your own way then. Are you quite sure,' he asked anxiously. 'you wouldn't rather do Mrs. Warren?'

'Yes,' said Tass.

The ticket collector came round.

'Sorry,' said Tass. 'Cleaned out.' She clambered off her ostrich.

'Me too,' said Peter. He left his lion. 'I told you it never stopped at sixpence,' he reminded Tass as they wandered off. The two small boys, still on the giraffe, gazed after them pathetically. Life was like that for brats.

'Off, you!' said the collector thumbing.

The small boys nodded sadly. They knew when argument was no good. But a bowler hat materialized from nowhere, if you could call the milling crowd that. It sat well above the ears, a sure sign of good humour.

'Let the nippers be, Joe,' said the Boss. 'I was young myself once.'

He stomped off. The collector gazed after him. He didn't believe it.

In spite of Betty Grable, the Ice Show, George Formby, George Doonan, Georgie Wood, and a myriad other attractions in watertight de luxes, Charley's Aunt opened to the biggest audience the Palookas at the Pavilion had played to on a Monday. It was quite a quarter full.

Having taken the plunge and gone lowbrow, Peter

Merrivale did it wholeheartedly. He had placarded the foot of the pier with hand-daubed posters announcing the Funniest Farce in the World, and the public, fresh from the the Fattest Woman in it (on show opposite), were in a mood to try anything once. Kids half price. What's more, once there they laughed at the dashing young undergrad in the old lady's bonnet. Takings mounted steadily. One more house like last night and they wouldn't be showing a loss. Tass felt a millionaire.

Friday night put them three pounds ahead and two shows on Saturday still to come! Unable to contain herself any longer, Tass dropped into the Boss' office to swank about it. She found him with his hat about half-way to his ears— routine Saturday morning mood. But sighting Tass he eased the hat a little higher and nodded.

'You here again lass,' he said. 'I'll make you a final offer. Twenty pounds and your fare back to London.'

'Keep it,' said Tass airily. 'We're doing fine.'

The bowler hat dropped a little.

'Beats me how you're still here and paying your rent,' said the Boss. 'I know that Joe of yours hadn't a penny in the bank ten days ago. Where did he get it from, lass?'

'From me,' said Tass airily. She leaned back and lit a cigarette. 'I'm in Management now. Here—have one?'

The Boss waved aside the Woodbines. He pressed down the bowler.

'So it's you, lass. It's your money. Didn't know you had any.'

'I haven't now,' said Tass.

'H'm,' said the Boss.

'But it's going to be all right,' said Tass. 'We've played to a profit.'

'You have!' said the Boss, both shaken and impressed.

'You were right about one thing,' said Tass. 'Hoy likes a laugh. We're keeping Charley's Aunt on for a second week. And,' she couldn't hold it back, 'we've got over ten pounds in advance bookings already. How's that?'

'Rotten,' said the Boss. He jammed his bowler right down and brooded at her.

'So it's your bit of money, lass,' he said. 'I'm sorry about that.'

'Oh, you don't have to worry,' said Tass lightly. 'I've got a little gold mine. Why don't you drop in and see us, Boss? I'll give you a complimentary if we've got an empty seat.' She rubbed her hands.

'Feeling good, eh?' said the Boss.

'Fine,' said Tass.

'Got any money left?'

'No,' said Tass.

'You haven't shown much sense, have you lass?'

'No,' said Tass.

'That you haven't,' said the Boss. 'Put all your eggs in one basket, haven't you?'

'But what a basket!' said Tass. She patted his shoulder gently, almost with affection and strolled out.

Her grandfather gazed at the door through which she had gone. He looked after her a long time. Then he reached for the telephone.

'Is that you, Joe?' he asked. 'Put the lights out on Hoy Haven Pier to-night—that's what I said. Hoy Haven Pier goes dark to-night and every night, till I tell you different. No—she's not closed down. She's there to go on for those that want to—in the dark.' He frowned. 'Joe,' he said dangerously, 'I didn't get that word " Canoodling"!'

He hung up. Anyhow, he reflected, canoodlers wouldn't be going in to see Hedda.

And that was that. On Thursday morning Tass arrived at the Boss' office to tell him so. She was considerably calmer than if she had rushed there on Saturday night as she wanted to.

'You old basket,' she said. 'You've beaten us. Now I suppose you're happy.'

'That's right,' said the Boss. The hat was well down and he looked glummer than ever. 'You made me keep my favourite pier dark, you cost me God knows how much money—not to speak of prestige—that whelk stall alone was a little gold mine. You've given me more headaches than I ever had in Hoy, and all because you wouldn't behave like reasonable people and go when I asked you.'

'That's right,' said Tass.

'And you've lost your bit of money?'

'That's right,' said Tass.

'Well, you've got to clear out now.'

'That's right,' said Tass. 'Going to make us an offer?'

'You're in no position to haggle over offers,' said the Boss strongly. 'You've got to take what I give you now.' He pondered. 'I'll pay your fares back to London, and that's more than I meant to do.'

'First class,' stipulated Tass.

'Third,' said the Boss. 'I've never travelled first in my life.'

'You're a generous winner, I must say,' said Tass. Her look was a spit.

'A generous winner is a fool,' said the Boss. 'All he does is set his foe on his feet again. How much did you put in, lass?'

'Eighty pounds,' said Tass. 'What's it to you?'

'I'll give you seventy,' said the Boss, 'and it's a cheap lesson at a tenner.'

'You'll give me eighty,' said Tass, 'or I won't take a penny. Either your conscience is biting you, or it isn't.'

'Seventy-five,' said the Boss. 'And it isn't my conscience. It's because you're a plucky lot of youngsters and I wish you well—everywhere except in Hoy.'

'Eighty,' said Tass.

'Seventy-nine,' said the Boss. 'You got to pay for your lesson. It's a law of nature.' He picked up a pen and started to write slowly and elaborately on a sheet of notepaper. 'And you'll sign this letter right now.'

'What's in it?' asked Tass.

'An undertaking to clear out of Hoy on Sunday,' said the Boss. 'And you don't get your fares back if you don't.'

'Oh, I'll sign it,' said Tass. 'Got to. But what's the hurry?'

'You'll see,' said the Boss. He handed her the pen and pointed a stubby finger. 'Sign,' he said.

[vii]

You'll see, the Boss had said. And that night Tass did. So did Hoy Haven and Hoy Beck and all the Saucy Belles plying on the sea between them.

Hoy Haven Pier had come out of the dark. The lights twinkled and the band played, the skittles rolled, the skaters revolved, faces of all ages smothered themselves in pink sugar beards, the Fun Fair was a clangour of pennies and all the booths were busy.

'Whelks,' roared the whelkman. 'They're lov-er-ly. Two-pence a saucer, and you don't need your ration books. 'Ere you are, Madam. Same again, sir? Just a minute, ma, I only got one pair of 'ands.'

The Boss' favourite pier was itself again.

At the Pavilion, Charley's Aunt broke its own record. Over half full and everyone laughing.

On Friday, the takings went up another seven pounds, and on Saturday Peter Merrivale found himself looking at a dust-covered board which read 'STANDING ROOM ONLY,' and wondering whether he would have to hang it out. He didn't, but it was a near thing.

So the Palookas at the Pavilion took their final curtains, part elated and part depressed and later straggled down the pier, their make-up still on their faces, part jubilant and part regretful, for a last sentimental saucer of nauseating whelks.

It was a relaxed whelkman who passed up the saucers.

'I hear you're going, Sir,' he said, 'and there's no one sorrier than I am. Put that purse away, Miss—it's on the House. It's a pity you couldn't tide over, Sir, it's a real pity you couldn't tide over. Vinegar, Miss? You'd have had a little gold mine here, Sir, if you could've hung on. A real little gold mine. . . .'

'We've had a good week,' said Peter. 'Blast him,' he added unaccountably.

But the whelkman followed this with ease. 'Wonder what you did to rile him?' he said. 'What's he got against you?'

'We're not the Pierrots,' said Peter.

'Ah,' said the whelkman profoundly. 'But you had a good show this week they tell me.'

'A jolly good show,' said Wilfrid Wilbraham, suddenly coming to life. 'And a jolly good week. And a jolly good season. And a jolly sight better one wherever we are next year.'

'That's right,' said Tass. 'Let's celebrate. Let's go on the roundabouts. What's sixpence?'

'It never stops at sixpence,' said Peter.

'Who cares?' said the Wisp. 'You're right, Tass. Let's say good-bye to Hoy the way Hoy was meant to be said good-bye to. We'll never be coming back here.' she said happily, 'that's certain.'

'That's right,' said Tass. 'We won't.'

'Come on, Rosie,' said Wilfrid Wilbraham, slapping the majestically munching Mrs. Bracegirdle on the rump. 'I bet nobody can guess your weight within a pound.'

'It couldn't matter less,' said Rose la Fleur.

It was a Saturday night and there was a queue at the roundabout. Of course. The Palookas from the Pavilion stood in it contentedly. They were laden with Presents from Hoy, miscellaneously collected by individual prowess. They were full of sickly lemonade and they were sugar-bearded to a performer.

Presently they were rising and falling and singing their heads off to the music of the roundabout, their make-up melting on their faces, with the coloured searchlights playing over them.

[viii]

'Blast the Boss,' said Peter Merrivale.

He was staring moodily through the grimy third-class

c

window of the London train at the sliding-back posters welcoming him to Hoy.

'Oh, forget him,' said Tass. 'He wasn't so bad.'

'He did for us all right,' said Peter.

'What I want to know,' said the Wisp, 'is where do we go from here?'

'To the Robinson Family,' said Wilfrid Wilbraham, back to normal.

'I don't know what you're complaining about,' boomed Lady Bountiful. 'We've had a nice time by the sea to set us up for the winter, we've been kept out of mischief and we've profited from the experience.' She toyed lovingly with a Victorian lorgnette. 'What's more, we've been paid our salaries, and frankly,' finished Rose la Fleur, 'that's more than I expected.'

Peter Merrivale grinned. 'Me too,' he said.

'There's a hall at Southend,' said Tass. 'It used to be the Congregational. Then they made it a Rest Centre. I wonder what's happened to it now?'

'Southend,' said Peter. He tasted the town.

'Third turning on the left off the High Street, then left again,' said Tass. 'We ought to be able to get it cheap.'

'With what?' asked Peter.

'With eighty pounds,' said Tass. 'Seventy-nine,' she corrected herself.

Wilfrid Wilbraham made a profound observation.

'Southend,' he said, 'is an hour's run from London.'

'Bill Bluebird pops down there quite often,' said the Wisp. 'Stays at the Palace,' she added knowledgeably.

'So does James Agate,' said Wilfrid Wilbraham.

The company brightened.

'I've got a sister at Southend,'' said Rose la Fleur, 'she runs a boarding-house.'

'The Company brightened still more. All except Wilfrid Wilbraham.

'What sort of boarding-house?' he enquired cautiously.

'Number two tours,' said Rose la Fleur.

'Ah,' said Wilfrid Wilbraham relieved. 'What's the capacity, Tass?'

'We could put on Anna Christie,' said the Wisp.

'We could put on Tug-Boat Annie,' said Annie. She spat.

'We could put on Mrs. Warren,' said Peter.

'We'll put on Charley's Aunt,' said Tass firmly. 'And after that While Parents Sleep, and then, when we've got money in the bank we can think about Hay Fever.

'We'll get the agents down,' said Wilfrid.

'We'll get the West End managements down,' said the Wisp.

'We'll get the critics down,' said Peter. 'Though not with your programme-building, Tass,' he pointed out. 'Still, I'll have my own play finished by then,' he gloried.

'Southend!' said Rose la Fleur. 'Very bracing.'

'And no Boss to beggar us out of it,' said Wilfrid.

'Oh, I don't know,' said Tass. 'He gave us a lunch basket, and that wasn't in the bargain.'

'Wonder what's in it?' mused the Wisp.

'Galantine sandwiches and beer,' said Wilfrid.

'I'm thirsty,' said the Wisp. 'Get it down.'

But it was chicken and champagne. The company staggered, then pounced.

'Two bottles,' said Rose la Fleur unbelievingly.

'Two chickens!' said the Wisp.

The very sight made them merry. They tore the chickens

limb from limb, they poured libations, they toasted one another and everybody they could think of. They toasted the whelkman, they toasted the landladies, they toasted Bill Bluebird.

'Here's to Southend,' toasted Bacchante.

'Here's to Hoy Haven,' said Wilfrid.

'And here's to the Boss,' said Peter Merrivale. 'Blast him.'

'I wonder if he's got any hair?' said Tass.

[ix]

'No, Joe,' said the Boss. 'Not more than ninepence. Wouldn't be value for money.'

'But we charged ninepence last year,' said Joe, whose name was Alf. 'And prices is up everywhere.'

'Not at Hoy, Joe,' said the Boss. 'Not while I can keep them down, anyway.'

He adjusted his bowler hat and stomped off, a solitary spender in the sharp April sunlight, leaving the owner of the Dodgem Cars to blaspheme mildly at his back, now advancing sturdily into the Haunted House.

The Boss was making his annual tour of Pleasure Beach on the day before it opened. He was no younger, no less flexible and in no better temper than he had been last year, and he disliked the thought of the stomach-turning switchback every bit as much. And like last year he put it off until after lunch.

There was little new on Pleasure Beach this season. Niagara Falls would have to wait till next summer—couldn't get the permits through. 'That's what comes of having that damned government,' he told a jumping-out skeleton.

The skeleton rattled its chains. Corny, thought the Boss.

Past the Fortune Teller—the Boss could take his palm as read. Fortune Tellers were always value for money; the more you paid the more you believed what they told you and the better value you got. Past the Derby. The horses had a new coat of paint—pretty! But it showed up the dingy grandstand. Slipshod.

'I was going to give it another coat to-night, Boss,' said the owner glibly.

Past the African Village—niggers not yet arrived. Only Joe practising the tom-tom—very bad he was at it too. Past the Chinese Laundry—after lunch. To four-rings-for-threepence, and no Present from Hoy after the lot of them. Getting old! Getting past it!

'Four more,' the Boss said grimly. He paid again.

Blast! Better pass on before he was ruined.

The Leaning Tower of Pisa. The Boss sought its isolation gratefully. He allowed himself to ascend by lift.

It was better up here. Hoy glittered and shone and gloried up at him. Hoy was a beauty, however you looked at her.

There was the Louis Quinze. That was the Red Mill—shouldn't have put it there. Where was the Palace of Art? Where was it? Vanished in the night! Wonderful! Oh, no, there was the great darn ugly thing. Might have known it.

There were his three piers stretching out into the sea—one, two, three. And there were his four Skylarks, lying on the beach ready to ply between them.

The Boss pulled out his field-glasses and ran his eyes along the gaunt Victorian skeleton of his favourite pier.

The whelk stall—a little gold mine. The skating-rink, like a hollow-glass wedding-cake. The windscreened bandstand—nice for invalids. Skittles—no matter how much you knocked them down you never wore them out. The Extension, free to all who cared to walk on it.

And at the Pavilion—the Pierrots. As they should be.

Larry Lance's La-di-das. Something to look forward to.

Unaccountably, the Boss sighed. He stowed away his field-glasses. He jammed down his bowler hat.

'To Hell with Hedda,' he comforted himself.

Shorty and Goliath

[Based on a theme by Herbert W. Victor]

IT was the year of the Earl's Court Exhibition and all London was going there by hansom. In the Portobello Road, the old Red Lion was hung with flags. Ladies with large hats and veils sat sipping their port and showing a dainty ankle. The men were cursing the war—the Franco-Turkish one.

'On me,' said Shorty.

'No,' said Goliath. 'On me.' He plonked down an opulent twopence and the barmaid hopped to it.

'To Emma,' said Shorty. He drank.

'And here's to the man she's going to marry,' said Goliath. Shorty considered this.

'Here's to him,' he agreed.

'Me,' said Goliath swigging.

Shorty put down his glass. 'No,' he said quietly. 'Me.'

The prettiest girl in Portobello Road was scooping out a pound of new potatoes. In the little living-room at the back of the shop the father was interviewing two of her suitors.

He poured out a glass of port. 'How much do you earn?' he said. He drank it.

Goliath shrank a little.

'Well,' he admitted, 'last week I had thirty-three and ninepence.'

Shorty swallowed. 'I didn't make as much,' he confessed. 'In fact,' he paused to break it gently, 'I got the sack.'

The greengrocer sat considering. As the bottle of port dwindled his thoughts took shape.

'You're good lads,' he said. 'Why, I've known you both since you were so high.' He held his hands at different levels. 'But the man that marries my Emma has got to show he's got it in him. He'll have the shop after I've gone.'

The thought saddened him. He produced another bottle.

'Don't take it hard, my lads,' he said. 'Have a drink with me and cheer up.'

They had several, but only the greengrocer grew more cheerful.

'You're good lads,' he said. 'I'm going to give you both a chance. How much money have you got?'

Goliath emptied his pockets. Shorty didn't need to.

The greengrocer took Goliath's money and gave him back tenpence.

'Now,' he said, 'you're starting level. And if one of you can walk into this shop to-morrow morning with a fiver in his pocket he can have my little Emma.'

A fiver! It was the Bank of England.

Outside the door the prettiest girl in Portobello Road removed her ear from the keyhole. Which of them did she want to win? Goliath was so resourceful—but she could make Shorty happy just by smiling at him.

What a dilemma!

On the pavement Shorty and Goliath shook hands.

'So long, old pal,' said Goliath, 'and remember there'll always be a place for you at my table.' He swaggered off.

But Shorty was hopeful too. He tilted his bowler hat and looked round for opportunity.

It was a lovely day. The sun was shining and there was music in the air. A barrel-organ was playing 'The Man who Broke the Bank at Monte Carlo.' Shorty approached. The monkey, a diagnostician if ever there was one, didn't even bother to hold out his cap.

ONE HUNDRED POUNDS REWARD!
    A pearl necklace . . .

Shorty looked at the notice. One hundred pounds! It didn't exist!

A man came running round the corner. He cannoned into Shorty and dived down an alleyway.

Shorty stared. The gentleman had dropped a parcel. He picked it up and ran down the alley after him. But the gentleman had run very fast and he was nowhere to be seen. So Shorty took the parcel to the Lost Property Office.

'Your name and address, please?' said the clerk. He wrote them down. 'Wait here a minute,' he said, and went behind the glass panel to open the parcel.

Shorty caught sight of the clock on the wall. He remembered his time was money. He dashed out.

'Hey!' cried the clerk re-emerging. He was dangling a pearl necklace.

But Shorty was half-way upstairs an Employment Agency.

The clerk at the Employment Agency was not very hopeful. 'Five pounds in a day!' He shook his head. 'Why, I don't even earn that myself!'

Now while Shorty was shouldering his disappointment his landlady was getting a shock. A motor car had exploded to a stop outside her respectable front door and a lady with a feather boa and a large pearl necklace was giving her a hundred pounds.

'A reward,' she said, 'for honesty.'

She climbed back into the car and exploded off.

The landlady hurried upstairs to give Shorty his hundred pounds, collect five weeks' back rent and make an apt comment about a feather. But the room was empty.

Shorty was out trying to earn a fiver.

The landlady made the bed. Her tenant was a millionaire. What a pity she had threatened to kick him out this morning!

Outside a fashionable gambling-house the carriages were beginning to roll up. Shorty had an inspiration. He dashed up and opened a carriage door and the toff, alighting, tossed him a sixpence.

A tanner! Shorty was enchanted. At this rate he had only to open—how many carriage doors was it?—and : . . He made a dash for a carriage and pair that might well be worth a bob.

A practised hand shoved him aside.

'Buzza you off,' said the powdered footman in his best English and looked his contempt at the crestfallen usurper. He looked again and his expressions changed. 'Mio Bambino,' he said. 'Shorty,' he translated. He embraced him.

Shorty blushed. 'Whatcher, Spaghetti,' he said embarrassed. 'How goes it?'

Spaghetti patted his gold-squiggled uniform. 'Magnifico,'

he said. 'I no peddle the ice-creama any more. I have the job.' He kissed his fingers. 'Come—I showa you.'

Together they went into the house, leaving the carriage and pair worth a bob to open the door for itself.

'Faites vos jeux,' said the croupier. A shower of gold placed itself carefully about the green baize. There was also a sixpence on Number Seven. It belonged to Shorty.

'Numero Sept,' said the croupier.

He paid out the gold. He looked at the sixpence. He blinked. But he was a good croupier. He paid out the sixpence.

'What do I do now?' asked Shorty, raking in the silver with trembling fingers and quite forgetting his original stake still on Number Seven.

'You getta you out,' said Spaghetti. 'Dam-quick. Here comma da boss.'

He bustled him through the door.

'Numero Sept!' said the croupier. That sixpence again!

Shorty staggered down the street lost in a financial daydream. Seventeen-and-sixpence had grown on a tree.

'My man!' A beaky old lady leant out of a fourth-floor window and pointed a parasol at him. 'Do you want to earn a shilling?'

Shorty earned it, trudging up four flights of stairs and slithering down again under three trunks, and a parrot.

And as he tugged and sweated, and the old lady scolded and the cabby swore and the parrot pecked, two men walked past carrying a wooden coffer. It contained a thousand golden sovereigns and they were taking them to Shorty's lodgings. There had been a run on Numero Sept.

The gaming-house had a reputation to keep up. So they had asked for the address of the man in the bowler hat, and when they learnt it they sacked Spaghetti for letting him in. Back to da hokey-pokey!

'Potatoes! Lovely and hot! Two a penny—potatoes!'

Shorty approached the burning brazier. Time was money, but, after all, he had to keep his strength up.

But as the vendor sprinkled salt, a cottage loaf in a rusty black shawl came plodding round the bend, sighted Shorty, and made for him. It was his landlady.

His rent! And he had nineteen-and-fourpence she could get off him!

Shorty grabbed the potato and made off. Nice state of things, he reflected as he ran, when you had to dodge your landlady out of doors as well as in.

Brandishing an umbrella, the landlady gave chase. Nice state of things, she reflected, when a lodger wouldn't wait to learn he was a millionaire.

It cost money to get through the turnstiles of the Earl's Court Exhibition, but Shorty knew the man at the gates. This gained him a lead while the landlady fumbled.

The Try-Your-Strength booth was doing a big business. 'Hit the bell and see a beautiful lady fall out of bed! Roll up! Roll up!' There were three beautiful ladies and four beautiful beds. The fourth beautiful lady had got tired and gone home with poppa.

Shorty grabbed the nightdress hanging at the back of the booth. He tied the ribbons of the nightcap under his chin. His landlady would never know him now.

Neither did the proprietor of the booth.

'Into bed, Gertie,' he ordered. 'What d'you think I pay you for?'

Pay! Shorty hopped.

Whang!

'Oh, Alf, that was lovely,' cooed the tobacconist's daughter as Shorty picked himself off the floor and climbed back into the bed. 'You got great strength.'

'Watch me do it again,' said Alf. He lifted the hammer. Whang!

The landlady came peering through the crowds. Girls in bed! Disgusting! She peered the other way.

Whang!

It was cool by the lake. Couples were drifting about in boats and, on shore, the band was playing the Valeta, and people were sitting at little tables, and dancing.

Bruised all over but with twenty-one and fourpence to jingle in his pocket, Shorty came sauntering to Emma and Goliath sitting at a table drinking sherbet.

'Who ho!' he said. 'How you doing?' And he thought of the twenty-one and fourpence in his pocket and he felt fine.

'Resting,' said Goliath. And he looked as though he could afford it.

The sun went behind a cloud.

'We been on the roundabouts,' said Emma. 'It was lovely. How you been doing?' she remembered.

'All right,' said Shorty and sat down carefully.

'Come and dance,' said Emma. But Shorty thought he wouldn't, so she danced with Goliath.

Shorty watched the dancers. But after a bit he got tired of smiling at Emma when she came round, and went back to wondering how much money Goliath had got in his wallet. It looked mighty plump, sticking out of the coat he had left on the arm of his chair. One little tilt and it would fall into the lake.

Did leather sink?

Emma came round and smiled and waved and was engulfed. Shorty couldn't see her—what's more she couldn't see him. His elbow sneaked out. A man could have an accident. Nobody could prove it wasn't an accident. Nobody would know.

'I'd know,' said Shorty's better self.

Shorty moved away, looked straight ahead of him and kept his elbows well in.

Emma and Goliath came back. Goliath mopped his brow, flopped into his chair and knocked his wallet into the water.

Leather did sink! For Emma gave a little shriek. Goliath gave a louder one.

'My money,' he mourned. 'All my money.'

With a sigh Shorty dived in. What else could he do? Goliath couldn't swim.

Very wet and no richer, Shorty trudged down the Portobello Road. There was a fortune waiting for him at his lodgings, but he was going back to dry his suit. No good could come of catching pneumonia.

But as he drew near the parlour window flew open and his landlady leant out and began to shout at him.

Twenty-one-and-fourpence! Better wet than penniless.

Shorty turned and ran.

Round the corner three large gents were looking at a small skylight. It was set at the back of a jeweller's shop. Shorty cannoned into them. They looked at Shorty.

'He'll do,' they said.

But Shorty dug in his heels. Any other night, he said, he'd climb through the skylight for three gents who had lost their key, with pleasure. But to-night, he said, was different. To-night, he said, his time was money. To-night he had to earn three pounds eighteen and eightpence.

'We'll give it to you,' said the three large gents.

They shouldered him up.

'Don't make a noise,' they warned him. 'Baby is asleep.'

So Shorty climbed down into the darkened hall, and very quietly opened the front door and extended his hand for payment.

But the three gents brushed past him, took out their tools and went to work on a safe.

'Forgotten the combination,' they told Shorty. Then they thrust a tray into his hand and began to load it with jewels.

Shorty was not a quick thinker, but he could get there.

'Blimey!' he said. 'You're burglars.'

'That's right,' said the three gents cordially. 'And so are you.'

'Cor,' said Shorty. He backed. He backed into a burglar alarm. It functioned.

Like three large streaks of lightning the three gents made for the door. Shorty, the tray in his hands, got through a bad fourth. A candlestick came wavering towards him. Shorty thrust the tray at the figure looming behind, ducked, and unencumbered, fled down the streets towards the bustling safety of the Earl's Court Exhibition.

Presently the police arrived. The jeweller showed them the loaded tray.

'Everything is saved,' he said, 'thanks to Shorty. What courage!'

The sergeant nodded. 'Frightened them off,' he said. 'Plucky.'

'And chasing them,' said the jeweller impressed. 'I'm going to reward that boy. Didn't lose his head.'

Once through the turnstiles, Shorty joined the sauntering throng. They were sauntering towards a booth. Outside there was a poster depleting a fist in a defiant attitude. Underneath was the challenge:

'FIVE POUNDS IF YOU CAN STAY THREE ROUNDS WITH THIS.'

Five pounds! Shorty tugged at his tie, swallowed twice, and marched himself in.

In the dressing-room a fat man in a sweater put Shorty into trunks and strapped a pair of boxing gloves on his hands. Shorty could hear the roar of the crowds through the curtains—then a thud. A moment later a man was carried in on a stretcher.

'Who's that?' asked Shorty.

'You're on next,' said the man in the sweater.

He trundled Shorty into the ring.

A sea of faces! Shorty managed to bow to them. He didn't half feel a fool. He didn't half feel chilly. He was glad Emma couldn't see him.

Blimey!

Goliath didn't ought to have brought a nice girl—not to a boxing match. Come to that, why wasn't Goliath having a go hisself?

Shorty's opponent came into focus.

He was!

'Seconds out,' said the referee.

They shook hands.

'Sorry, old pal,' said Goliath. 'I gotta do it.'

He socked him.

Shorty got off the stretcher and sat on a chair while the man in the sweater undid his boxing gloves.

'Cheer up, chum,' he said. ' 'Taint everyone's cut out to be a fighter.'

Shorty thought it over. He nodded.

There was a flurry outside the door. Emma dodged her way in. She knelt down beside Shorty. The man in the sweater looked the other way.

'All this for me,' said Emma, touching his bruised cheek.

'No, Emma,' he said. 'I bin thinking. I won't do. Not for you, Emma.'

'Oh, Shorty,' said Emma.

'You better marry Goliath,' said Shorty. 'He could look after you.'

Goliath came in. He looked a little sheepish.

'Sorry, old man,' he said.

'That's all right,' said Shorty. 'See you at the wedding.' He walked out.

You could get an awful lot of whisky for twenty-one and fourpence.

When Shorty came out of jail his landlady had stopped looking for him out of the window. So Shorty trudged up to his attic unobserved and lay on the bed.

Somebody had moved the dead geranium from the bamboo table by the window and put a wooden box there instead. Indignantly Shorty rose to investigate.

One hundred golden sovereigns in the wash-basin—a reward for honesty.

Fifty golden sovereigns in the tooth-glass. From the grateful jeweller.

One thousand golden sovereigns in the wooden box. He'd won it. Him!

On the mantelpiece was a picture postcard. It showed a pair of happy honeymooners at Clacton-on-Sea. Shorty turned it over. Emma and Goliath.

'Having a wonderful time,' it read.

Shorty crossed to the window and gazed into the street. A pack of kids were playing hop-scotch. Idly Shorty picked up a golden sovereign and threw it to them. The kids took no notice.

He threw another.

One of the kids ran after it and came back gloating. The others crowded under the window and looked at Shorty appealingly.

Something came over Shorty. He dug his hands into the casket as far as they would go and cast the gold out of the window.

Suddenly the Portobello Road became very full outside Shorty's house. People were scrambling in the gutters. Others were running up.

Shorty went on throwing, quicker and quicker, more and more. When the casket was empty he turned to the basin and tilted that. Then he threw the tooth-glass and the golden rain was over.

Flushed with exhausted triumph, Shorty turned. Arms akimbo, his landlady was straddling the doorway.

'Fine goings on,' she said. 'I'll trouble you for my rent.'

His rent! Triumph ebbed.

' 'Arf a mo,' said Shorty.

He ran down to the street and scrambled with the others.

Stroganoff, Said the Duchess

IT was a beautiful summer's morning in Mayfair; that is
to say no one so far had risked a hundred pound fine by
turning on the electric fire, even behind blinked blinds.

Caryl Haskell-Beaumont wandered elegantly into Deben-
ham's, rather quickly out again, and took a cup of Danish
coffee in Wigmore Street.

Blast! Only a quarter to eleven.

Into the Times Book Club. What a pile of Trudi Trumps!
Not only did they not seem to have sold any, but somebody
must have brought some back.

'Sticky,' said the saleswoman sympathetically.

Caryl Haskell-Beaumont, caught counting, started
guiltily. As usual, she pretended she had dropped in to buy
something.

'Have you the new-um-Priestley?'

Her luck held. They hadn't.

Past the Polytechnique—Mickey Mouse—tempting. But
not for another twenty minutes. Gorgeous Guana! That
settled it. On to the Café Royal Bar. Not open yet.

Ah!

With the greatest unconcern in the world Caryl Haskell-
Beaumont approached the newspaper-vendor. Only a

fellow-writer would have guessed, and guessed very easily, that here was the real object of this morning's odyssey. She ignored Palestine. She ignored the United States. She ignored whatever it was Russia wouldn't agree to. She turned the pages in search of the notice she had written last night under the influence of strong tea.

Last night the Ballet Stroganoff opened a six weeks' season at Covent Garden before a fashionable audience . . .

. . . 'Princess Elizabeth she come?' panted Stroganoff.

The bald-headed impresario had burst into the Press Room where Lord Streatham, the Public Relations Charmer, was pleading across the first-night seating plan with the cash-conscious Box Office Manager.

'But I can't put Lord Beaverbrook in the Upper Circle,' he was arguing.

'The Princess,' said Stroganoff anxiously. 'I hear the rumour terrible.'

Lord Streatham spared him a glance.

'It isn't a rumour,' he said. 'It's it.'

Stroganoff sat down heavily, appropriately enough on the seating plan.

'I'm sorry, old boy,' conceded Lord Streatham. 'I've done my best. Been 'phoning Biffo all morning.'

Stroganoff pondered. 'This Biffo,' he said. 'He is your friend?'

'We were at Harrow,' said Lord Streatham. He blushed.

'Bon,' said Stroganoff. 'Then you 'phone him again. You tell him that without the Princess you are the sack.'

'It wouldn't do any good,' said Lord Streatham. 'He says the Princesses had a basinful of ballet when Helpmann was here. D'you mind moving off, old boy?'

He pushed gently at the gesticulating bald-headed bulk. The bulk waved its arms at him.

'Why you push?' it demanded. 'Have I not troubles enough that you do not let me sit in my own theatre for which I pay the rent—or will do? Leave me to solve my problems in the silence utter. For twenty years,' he babbled on, 'I have tried to present my ballet at Covent Garden. I have made the plot, done the pinch, gone the bust, and got rich again, and only for Covent Garden. I have reculer myself from London to Kansas City *pour mieux sauter*—but instead I find that I have alight at Buenos Ayres where I have the difficulties enormous, for Arenskaya she decide suddenly she want to be white slave, but no one will have her though she get many offers as Madame . . .'

The Box Office Manager blinked.

'Do not ask me how I get to London?' said Stroganoff. He waited hopefully. . . . 'I tell you,' he volunteered. 'We dance in Yokohama and Arenskaya she put the eye on the American Commandant and he say you take our planes and you go to London dam quick. And here I am,' he flung out his arms, 'at Covent Garden, the capital of the world of ballet.'

'He is, you know,' said Streatham.

'I am at Covent Garden,' gloated Stroganoff. 'I have the ballet that every impresario wishes to present. Hylton he come to me on his knees. Littler offer me the advance, and also,' he remembered, 'the cigar. But because it is Covent Garden and because I have waited for it all my life I turn down the knees and I do not take the cigar and instead I sign the contract with the Webster One dam quick, and I do not even read Clause 123 which forbid me to sack the conductor, and Dourakova she buy a gun and Arenskaya she search for it all the time, though I tell her that she is childish for it is well known that Doura cannot shoot straight—else, bang! I should not be here,' he pointed out. 'What is it I am proving to you?' he asked.

'Prove it on the sofa, old boy,' said Lord Streatham. He tried a tentative push.

Stroganoff slapped down his hand. 'I remember now,' he said accusingly. 'The Princess—she does not come. My fashionable opening it is the slum.'

'Oh, I wouldn't say that,' said Lord Streatham. 'You'll get all the right people, you know.'

'Poof!' said Stroganoff violently.

'If only,' said Lord Streatham with charm, 'I can persuade this fellow here from giving all the best seats in the house to the directors and their friends.'

'The directors—yes,' said Stroganoff. 'The friends—no. Absolutely no,' he remembered. 'And anyways,' he announced, 'without the Princess there can be no opening at all.' He slid resolutely off the table. 'Which way,' he demanded, 'is the Palace Buckingham?'

'Don't tell him,' urged Lord Streatham with awful visions of Stroganoff assaulting the sentry floating before him. What's more he didn't put it past the old boy to get in. 'Relax, old man,' he urged. 'Come and sit on the table.' He smoothed out the plan temptingly.

But Stroganoff was firm. 'My friend,' he said, 'Soyez raisonable. Since you have fail me I must go to the Princess myself. At first,' he decided, 'she will be correct but cold— very cold, is she not an Englishwoman? But I will make her the argument eloquent, and presently we will be weeping together and then the mamoushka will arrive and ask what is the matter? And dry her eyes and offer to come to the opening too . . .'

'You're not to do it,' said Lord Streatham really alarmed.

'My friend,' said Stroganoff, 'it is my duty to my company. My company,' he declaimed. 'It looks on me as a father. It brings to the Pappa Vladimir all its troubles, its loves, its hates, especially,' he remembered fondly, 'its hates. And also it asks for the little risings. How,' he demanded, 'am I to give them the little risings if the Princess she do not come to the opening?'

'We might get the Duchess of Dumpshire,' mused Lord Streatham. 'Mind you,' he pointed out, 'she's difficult.'

'Duchess—poof!' said Stroganoff. ' 'Ow can I open with only a Duchess?'

'You opened without Benois 'imself once, remember?' said Box Office.*

'Then,' said Stroganoff coldly, 'I had the murder to help me. My poor Puthyk,' he remembered suddenly. 'To think I am already in London many days and have not yet been to visit him in that pretty asylum in Surrey. I go at once to take him some caviar. You have the account at Fortnum?' he asked Lord Streatham. He noted the dismayed reaction. 'Ah, bon,' he said.

He went.

'Now look here, old man,' said Lord Streatham to the Box Office, with charm, 'you can't put Lord Beaverbrook in the Upper Circle . . .'

*Who could have given him 'A Bullet in the Ballet' in exchange for a free seat in the Stalls–Circle? And how did he ever find time to read it?

At Fortnum and Mason's, the Duchess of Dumpshire was being difficult. Already she had reduced the charming smile of the soothing saleswoman to a strained expression on a Lizzie Arden face and was now striving for the same effect on the much tougher proposition of the Departmental Shock Absorber. She liked her caviar as much as anyone, but she disliked having to pay ten guineas a jar for it. So now she turned aside to ask the price of a can of asparagus just to give herself the pleasure of refusing to buy it.

But when, this pleasure achieved, she turned back to the caviar, she found it was being clutched by a bald dome with a watch-chained stomach, who was telling the Liz Arden expression to charge it to Lord Streatham and ring him up if she didn't believe him. Really, the friends Tiny Streatham had!

'My jar,' said the Duchess majestically. She extended a hand and waited.

Nothing happened.

'My jar,' said the Duchess. 'You must have seen me pick it up.'

'I have also seen you put it back,' retorted Stroganoff. He hugged it more closely.

'It is the last jar,' said the Liz Arden expression. It sounded as though it was the last straw.

'We're expecting another consignment to-morrow,' said the Shock Absorber soothingly.

'Poof!' said Stroganoff.

'Quiet,' said the Duchess. 'Now then, sir,' she turned to Stroganoff, 'are you going to give me that jar or do I send for the police?'

The Liz Arden expression disintegrated. The Shock

Absorber vanished, presumably in search of a higher-up Buffer. But Stroganoff was one vast beam.

'The police,' he said. 'I am well known to your English police.'

'No doubt,' said the Duchess drily.

'I have done much for this Scotland Yard of yours,' Stroganoff wagged a pleased head. 'For many weeks I keep them in the headlines with the bullets in my ballet. Ah—that Adam Quill—quel beau garcon!' He released a finger from the clutched jar to kiss it and quickly curled it round again. 'Mind you,' he said, 'he do not understand the ballet very well, and I do not think he is the very good detective but he has the rich old aunt who give him money though it will be better when she die and he have it all.'

'I,' said the Duchess, 'am the rich old aunt, and I haven't the slightest intention of dying.'

'Entendu,' said Stroganoff, who had not been listening. Indeed, he was off on a delightful daydream of his own. 'When M'sieur Quill is rich,' he announced, 'my troubles will be over. "Pappa Stroganoff," he will say, for I am to him as a father, you understand . . .'

The Duchess didn't. She made a feeble grab at the jar, Stroganoff parried it in his stride and went on.

' "Pappa Stroganoff," he will say, "what shall I do with all this lovely money that the old aunt who is dead at last, may her soul rest in peace, has left me?" "Mon ami," I will say, "what simpler? You put it in my ballet." And M'sieur Quill,' he beamed, 'he put.'

A good thing the Foreign Office had sent her nephew to South America reflected the Duchess. Adam was quite capable of putting money in a ballet company if he could

TO HELL WITH HEDDA!   88

get his hands on it. And that reminded her. She made a
sudden pounce at the jar and won.

'This was not nice,' said Stroganoff hurt. 'I make you the
little confidence and you snatch my caviar. You give me
back please,' he pleaded. 'It is not for me but for my poor
Puthyk, who is quite mad.'

'It seems to me, sir,' said the Duchess coldly, 'that you
must be insane yourself.'

She gathered up her sable stole, her sunshade, her lorgnette, the stiff folds of the last bombazine skirt in London,
and her caviar and swept out—a monumental institution of
beaky dignity.

'Eh bien,' said Stroganoff, 'I take the asparagus. And
maybe some grapes. And also,' he remembered, 'a water-
melon. The strawberries?' he pointed. ' 'Ow mooch? No
matter, I take . . .'

Late that sunny afternoon a tall elegant shadow strolled
leisurely along Park Crescent accompanied by a rotund,
carnationed, and hurrying to keep pace blob.

Streatham and Stroganoff were on their way to take tea
with the Duchess of Dumpshire to invite her to attend the
opening performance at Covent Garden.

'Now for God's sake don't rattle the old girl, old man,'
said Lord Streatham.

'Moi,' said Stroganoff. 'Rattle! Always you take me for
the baby,' he complained.

'Just keep smiling and nodding,' said Lord Streatham,
'and leave me to do the talking. And don't take a second
slice of anything. Nothing annoys old Angie more. Not
that there'll be much, anyway.'

'I'm hungry,' said Stroganoff.

'Oh dear.' said Lord Streatham. 'Stay hungry,' he urged, as he tugged at the doorbell.

A footman ushered them upstairs. There were a great many tables, none of them spread. And there was Angela Dumpshire looking displeased already.

'Hallo, hallo, hallo,' said Lord Streatham. 'Here we are—what!'

'Quiet, Tiny,' said the Duchess. She lifted her lorgnette from *The Times* and inspected the bristling bald dome. 'So you are Stroganoff,' she said. 'I might have guessed it.'

'So it is you—the Duchess,' said Stroganoff. 'How could I guess it? What you do with my caviar?' he changed the subject to a happier theme.

'What's it to do with you?' snapped the Duchess. 'I'm having it for supper.'

'But me, I am here only for tea,' objected Stroganoff. 'It is not hospitable this,' he complained, 'after I give you with my own hands the last jar.'

'Give!' said the Duchess. 'I had to stand on tiptoe and snatch and you know it.'

'Well, well, well,' said Lord Streatham jovially, 'what have you two been up to?'

The two glares that had been engaged in a death grapple switched.

'Quiet, Tiny,' said the Duchess.

'Quiet,' hissed Stroganoff. 'Don't make her the rattle.' He turned back to the enemy. 'Let us not talk of the caviar any more,' he said largely. 'It was not very good caviar, anyway. . . .'

'Not good!' said the Duchess sidetracked. 'Ten guineas!'

'The grain's small,' explained Stroganoff. 'But, poof, it is good enough for the English for they do not understand the caviar and do not eat too much.' He squared his shoulders and bowed formally. 'Duchess,' he said, 'since the Princess she do not come, I have the honour to invite you to our opening performance.'

'And I,' said the Duchess, 'have the pleasure of refusing to go anywhere near it . . .'

. . . *The opening programme, announcements for which have so frequently been changed, turned out to be reasonably routine.* LES SYLPHIDES, BLACK MARKET, *and that classic piece of safety play,* AURORA'S WEDDING. . . .

'Non, non, non,' said Stroganoff explosively. 'Assez d'Aurore. The public is sick of Aurore. I am sick of Aurore. You are sick of Aurore.'

'Bien sur, I am sick,' said Arenskaya. 'And I am even more sick of the manner your company she dance it.'

This was a new gambit Arenskaya had recently discovered to infuriate Stroganoff. Whenever she now blamed the ballet it was his. Whenever she praised it, it was hers. It never failed to work.

'Me, I am the business man,' said Stroganoff hotly. 'It is you who direct the dancing.'

'Bon,' said Arenskaya. 'I direct that we give Aurore. How else,' she argued not without justification, 'can I give solos to all those little elephants whose mamoushkas you have promised or they give you the giffle.'

'This they do, anyway,' said Stroganoff, massaging a remembering cheek. 'But if we give Aurore what will Nevajno say?'

'And if we don't,' said Arenskaya, 'what will the Daughter of Doura say?'

It will be seen that building the programme for an opening night is something more than jabbing a pin into one's
repertoire, even though the result will frequently suggest
that it is little more. Pleasing the public is, of course, always
the major consideration, but it is apt to get mislaid among
the minor ones that come crowding in as the battle
develops.

One begins, correctly enough, with SYLPHIDES. The com-
poser is dead, the choreography is a classic, tulle is off
coupons, and anyone can find black curtains. You would
think the thing was simple to settle. And so it would be if
it were not always the first ballet in the programme and the
Ballerina Assoluta did not feel she would seem more
Assoluta if she postponed her appearance till the second.
This invariably leaves at least three ballerinas with about
equal claims to the star part and equally voluble mamoushkas
to state them.

Then there is the problem of the male dancer. Here there
is no glut but a definite shortage which will not be eased
until the wig is made more attractive and which, at present,
can only be overcome with bribes of little risings and other
inducements, some of them very strong. Add to this
opposing death grips on The Prelude, the transplantations
from the back row to the front row of the corps-de-ballet,
and the backer's little Baskova, and you will realize why, in
every planning, Sylphides is thrown out half a dozen times
only to come back because every other opening ballet is so
much more difficult to settle.

'Nobody will watch it, anyway,' they console each other
when finally it is pencilled in.

Then there is the New Work—the world première, with
all the critics trying to sneak into rehearsals to give them-

selves longer to make up their minds what to say about it. This New Work has one small point in its favour—it has definitely been decided to do it—if the orchestrations are ready in time, not to mention the choreography. But as against this you are likely to lose your classical ballerina, particularly if the choreographer has carelessly failed to provide for whatever it is she does best, or, worse, put in something that she no longer does so well.

At this point of programme planning somebody raises the question of the musical interlude. It is usually the conductor, who has either dug out something he rather fancies, or rearranged something else rather better, he thinks, or remembered one of his early works, never fully appreciated, he maintains, or merely feels it is bad policy not to exhaust the orchestra before the last work. Ranged against him are the Rose Spectres, whose leaps through French windows are threatened by the Time Factor, the crush bar, deeming that any curtailment in the crushing can only lead to un-eaten hors-d'œuvres, and all the ushers, with strict orders not to let anyone in while the performance is in progress and never able to obtain a ruling whether the Interlude with lowered lights counts. And, of course, the orchestra. But the conductor usually wins if only because he can make it so strenuous for the dancers if he doesn't.

After this there is only the last ballet to be decided. Theoretically the problem should not be insoluble. The main event of the evening is over. The critics have gone. All that is needed is some work to send the audience out to fight for taxis in a happy mood—(Prince Igor or Les Patineurs) or, alternatively in a mood of uncomprehending despair—(Adam Zero.)

But in practice, programme-building at this point

becomes the mamoushka's battleground, fought with un-fulfilled soloists across an insufficiency of solos, of which the Assoluta, who has Dunkirked herself out of Sylphides, now does a D-Day back, pointing out that so far she has only been given a *pas de deux* with variations and must have at least two if she is to remain with the company.

Then there are the choreographers, men of infinite talent and convinced of it, as temperamental as teething babies, as brittle as ballerinas, and just as jealous of each other even if they don't show it quite so much. Stroganoff solved this problem by having only one choreographer and relying on Arenskaya's memory for tatting up the classics. But when it came to storms in samovars, Nicolas Nevajno, choreo-grapher of the future, with the permanently overdrawn bank account was as good as a night in the bare mountains.

Now he came lividly into the room, his unruly black hair horribly slicked down with brilliantine. Absently he had brooded himself into a barber's shop and by the time he had discovered that the whole conception that had come to him while not buying heather from a gipsy, stank, the barber had done everything except get paid.

'What is it I hear?' he demanded. 'Me between Sylphides and Aurore? Never!'

'Mais Nicolas,' said Stroganoff. 'Soyez raisonable. We cannot have the Soirée Nevajno.'

'And why not?' asked the genius. He ran his hands through his hair. It began to look a little better.

'Doura would be difficult,' said Stroganoff with masterly understatement.

The image failed to register. 'But it is an idea this soirée Nevajno you propose,' said the Choreographer of the future. 'We start with Gare du Nord—the locomotive you will repaint—then my new conception Black Market, and for the end we revive Table d'Hôte. Yes,' he approved, 'the idea it has something.'

'It has the stink,' said Arenskaya. 'And also nowhere is there room for Doura to get on pointes.'

'There can be no pointes in Black Market,' said Nevajno loftily.

'Bien sur,' said Stroganoff. Having made the little joke he cackled at it.

'Then it is settle,' said Nevajno, 'and I go at once to instal myself at the Savoy to contemplate, so you schange me schmall cheque and arrange the guzzle for the press.'

'Tenez, tenez,' said Stroganoff. 'This Soirée Nevajno it is an idea perhaps, but it is not a good idea, voyons!'

'What is not a good idea?' said a voice in the doorway, sweet as honeysuckle, sharp as a razor blade in an advertisement.

It was the daughter of Doura. On the bills she was Drina Dourakova, but she was Doura's daughter everywhere else. Wonderful Doura. Sixty-five years old and still remembered in England in every notice her daughter got. Poor Drina—a slip of a ballerina of forty-one, still sharing her notices of Giselle with how much better her mother had been in it. Poor Stroganoff, never daring to remember the mother's performance to the daughter and never daring not to remember it to the mother. Lucky Arenskaya, who didn't give a nichevo what she said or who she said it to.

'Ah, the daughter of Doura,' she said now. 'Come in, my darling,' she welcomed, knowing well that here was an ally in the battle for appeasement solos that Stroganoff might be talked into abandoning. It was well known you could talk Stroganoff into abandoning anything but a backer.

'Come in, my darling,' she repeated, 'and listen to the idea that stinks.'

The daughter of Doura serpented over. She kissed Arenskaya distastefully on the cheek. She looked at Nevajno's slicked down hair.

'Why you wear a wig?' she demanded. 'It is horrible,' she decided.

Nevajno peered into the mirror. He staggered. He went to work with both hands.

'There, that is better,' he said. 'Now,' he relaxed, 'we discuss the details of our opening.'

'These I settle last night,' said Doura, mamoushka uppermost. 'With myself,' she explained. 'That is what I have come here to tell you. So you will send for the Webster One and tell him to announce,' she began to tick off on her fingers, 'Lac de Cygnes—Act two. Giselle—Act two. And the Sleeping Princess—Act three.'

The ally had vanished. Arenskaya threw up her hands.

'She has gone mad, the daughter of Doura,' she announced. 'I have been waiting for it a long time. Soon she foam at the mouth.' She folded her hands and waited.

Stroganoff, the diplomat, frowned at her. 'It is an idea,' he said ponderously, 'but,' he tried a wily appeal to reason, 'would the daughter break the tradition of the mother and dance the first ballet at a London opening? Aie! Why you do that?' he demanded puzzled, rubbing the cheek that Arenskaya had lunged out and giffled.

'You are about to see,' said Arenskaya ominously.

The daughter of Doura, a dew-drop on a porcupine, smiled sweetly.

'It will be a change for once to do something that my mother has not done,' she said.

'You were right,' said Stroganoff sadly. He slapped himself on the other cheek.

'Your mother,' said the choreographer of the future with an amazing turn of speed for one usually so abstracted, 'has never danced at a Soirée Nevajno.'

They were back where they had started.

'Now all it need,' said Stroganoff to the ceiling, 'is for someone to come in with another idea.'

The door opened. A boy with black boot-button eyes came in, drank in the scene, grinned at it, handed Stroganoff an unstamped envelope, grinned again, and went out.

'If I employ that one, I sack him,' said Stroganoff forcibly. He tore open the envelope. 'Mon Dieu,' he said, 'it is from the Webster One.'

'What have we done now?' asked Arenskaya.

'He has the suggestion for the opening,' said Stroganoff. 'He wishes we give Prince Igor with Rokovsky.'

'It is in our contract?' demanded Arenskaya.

Stroganoff pondered. 'I do not think so,' he said.

'Ah bon,' said Arenskaya. She grabbed the administrator's message out of his hand and threw it out of the open window, then they all moved over to watch it flutter down.

It was caught by a passing Spiv, who read it, lost interest, threw it in the gutter, and passed on.

'The public has spoken,' said Stroganoff impressed.

For a moment the company were united in approval, then:

'Concerning the Soirée Nevajno,' said the Choreographer.

'Concerning my opening ballets,' said the daughter of Doura.

'Concerning Le Marriage d'Aurore,' said Arenskaya more loudly than the other two.

The Backer came in, his little Baskova on his arm, a brand new bracelet on hers.

'Good morning,' he said shortly. 'My treasure here tells me that she hasn't got her ballet. Why?'

He had not made a fortune out of flour by finesse.

'Our little chick has no Ballet,' said Stroganoff in horror, who knew perfectly well the chick hadn't and wouldn't have if he could help it, whatever promises it might be tactful to make. 'I am astounded.' He opened his eyes to their widest extent. 'My Princess,' he turned reprovingly on Arenskaya, 'why have we not yet arranged a Ballet for our little chick?'

'Because she stink,' said Arenskaya, who had not won her position by finesse either.

The little chick burst into tears. The Backer fished in his pocket and hung a diamond pendant on her. She took time off to look and went back to her sobbing.

'If you hang it on her,' the daughter of Doura pointed to Arenskaya, 'it might be wiser.'

The room was electric with opposing glares of enmity. Into them pokered a beaky old lady of sixty-eight with a locket of her poor dead Tzar pinned firmly on her Molyneux.

'Vladimir,' she rasped. 'What is this madness I hear of a Soirée Nevajno? What is this plot against my publicity?'

'That settle it,' said Stroganoff firmly. 'I write to the Webster One and demand that the messenger boy is sack. He listen outside the door,' he explained unnecessarily.

'Do not distress yourself, Mamoushka,' said the daughter of Doura. 'I demand to open as we have agreed. My three ballets—or I do the walk out.'

'And I demand my soirée or I do the walk out,' said Nevajno.

'And I demand my Ballet,' hiccupped the blubbing Baskova.

'Or I walk out,' said the Backer.

'And I demand that we end with Aurore,' said Arenskaya, 'and maybe I do the walk out and maybe I don't.'

And they all turned to advance on what should have been a cowering Stroganoff.

But that diplomat had for once proved himself a true diplomat. He'd gone.

'The programme opened with Les Sylphides.' . . .

Caryl Haskell-Beaumont was a conscientious critic and never expressed an opinion on what she hadn't seen. And together with nearly all the other critics she had seen no reason to see the Sylphides Stroganoff. Indeed, the crush-bar counted on doing very nice business during the Sylphides Stroganoff.

There was the Webster One talking to the Ashton One. There were the critics standing each other drinks, passing the time away before they could decently go up to the press-room and be stood drinks by the management. There was the Valois One, a well-pleased poker, and there was Our Mim, circulating and gesticulating and forgiving the critics. There was Lord Streatham talking to everyone with

charm and there was everyone talking to Lord Streatham
with no charm and often a great deal of heat; there were the
décor boys, trying to be seen talking to Oliver. And of
course there were a certain number of people inside the
auditorium, but they had paid for their seats. And so Harry
the barman doled out the whiskies and looked benevolently
at the experienced faces for the moment happily relaxed,
prepared to endure later but not a moment before they must.

Into this pink-carpeted, crystal-chandeliered scene, shot a
bald dome mopping itself.

'Mon Dieu,' it announced to the assembly, 'the little
Baskova has just danced the Prelude preposterous.'

'Sssh,' said Lord Streatham.

'It was 'orrible,' said Stroganoff loudly.

'Sssh,' said Lord Streatham. 'The critics,' he hissed.
'Hello, hello, hello,' he said all round him, trying to drown
Stroganoff, 'well, well, well . . .'

'Mon Dieu!' said Stroganoff aghast at his own candour.
'The little Baskova,' he rallied much too late, 'she has
danced the Prelude like . . .' he could not bring himself to
speak the words but he managed to kiss his fingers.

Four rows of pearls and a made-over Worth came
screaming into the foyer and bore down on Stroganoff.

'It is the ruin,' screamed Arenskaya. 'It is the disaster.
You must be mad. Never can we hold up our heads again.'

They all crowded round to listen.

'I have watched many audiences in the Prelude,' said
Arenskaya. 'I have seen them weep. I have seen them sleep.
But never,' she announced, 'have I thought it possible that
I should hear them laugh out loud.'

'You exaggerate,' said Stroganoff. 'Maybe,' he conceded,
'they giggle a little but no more.'

'That,' said Arenskaya, 'was before she fall down.'

Caryl Haskell-Beaumont looked wistful. Maybe she had missed something after all.

'And it is you, Vladimir,' said Arenskaya, screaming once more, 'who insist that she dance. Did I not warn you? Did I not reason with you? Did I not threaten you with the suicide?'

'And also,' said Stroganoff mildly, 'with the murder.'

'Oh, hello—nice to see you!' Lord Streatham had grasped despairingly at the first person in sight. It turned out to be the Webster One. Unlucky.

'But no,' Arenskaya went on, 'you would not listen. Very well, but——' she quivered, 'it must not happen again.'

The Webster One looked sympathetic. But only for a moment. Then he frowned, stooped and picked up a smouldering cigarette that had burnt an undeniable hole in the rose-pink carpet.

'My darling,' said Stroganoff, 'I know you suffer, but have I not told you many times not to throw the burning cigarette on the Webster One's carpet?'

Arenskaya lit another. 'It is in our contract that we do not throw cigarettes on the carpet?' she demanded.

Stroganoff pondered. 'I do not think so,' he said.

'Ah bon,' said Arenskaya.

She threw it.

A thin spatter of applause came through the walls.

'The applause!' said Stroganoff. 'All is yet well.'

Galvanized he rushed off to swell it. Arenskaya rushed with him.

Sadly the non-smoking Webster One picked up the smouldering cigarette.

'Twopence!' he said. 'Just as if it grew on trees.'

. . . Nicolas Nevajno is called the choreographer of the future. He has been called it for the past twenty years. Why?

Black Market (music by Polyshumadshedshi, choreography, décor and costumes by Nevajno), presents the ballet-goer with this choreographer's usual problem. Either he is to believe his programme notes or he is to believe the evidence of his eyes. My programme told me that Black Market is the symbol of Man's struggle through the ages, his immortal yearnings, and an alley in Soho. The Black Market (Fate, Mammon, and a dancer) draws a glove—(the symbol of possession) from under the counter—(consolidated trusts). The Pure Young Prostitute (Drina Dourakova) takes up the glove and gives it to her lover (A Spiv-Plenty amid starvation—The Margin of Diminishing Returns)—to the great indignation of the Corps-de-Ballet (Mass Observation). After a furious osstinato the enemy, neither the performance nor the programme makes clear who this is, is routed and the Black Marketeer is confronted by his widowed mother (Doura Dourakova), curiously dressed for a ballet of the future in full Maryinski regalia and side-curls. While he too is staggering at the sight of her, she kills him so that mankind may be left free to go molested to its doom. Which it does round and round the stage to a neat display of Odeon lighting till the curtain comes down to the usual cat-calls that are now a part of the Nevajno first night tradition.

To many in the audience, including the American Whistle in the gallery, the point of outstanding interest in this premier was the reappearance of the Grand Old Lady of the Ballet, Doura Dourakova, as the Black Marketeer's Mum. It was a bold bid for leniency on Stroganoff's part to present the Dowager Queen of Ballerinas in this exacting part. . . .

. . . Doura Dourakova looked indignant. 'Useless to argue, Vladimir,' she said. 'I have decided that I wish to dance

again and all my life,' she pointed out quite correctly, 'I have
done as I wished.'

'But your 'eart,' said Stroganoff. 'Remember how you
always have the little attack when I have the little argumenta-
tion with Drina that she could not win without. What will
'appen to your 'eart just before the curtain it go up?'

'It will go boom,' said Dourakova placidly, 'as it has so
often done before and my knees will tremble a little but I
will take my stage as I have always done.'

'But, my darling,' pleaded Stroganoff. 'What will you do
when you have taken it? You cannot do the thirty-two
fouettes any more. You could not do them fifteen years
ago,' he pointed out.

'I would have done them but for the conductor,' said
Dourakova coldly. 'Mais, alors, are there to be circus tricks
in the new Nevajno?'

'You wish to dance in Black Market?' said Stroganoff
horrified.

'Bien sur,' said Dourakova.

The idea had come to her that morning when her
American airmail had included several press cuttings, com-
menting on Tchernitcheva's reappearance in Sheherazade.
Immediately she had hopped out of bed, clutched the bed-
rail, and tried a plié.

'My darling,' said a silvery imperial in the bed, 'what 'as
happen?'

'Quiet, idiot,' said the divine Dourakova, 'is this the first
time that you have seen me limber up?'

The imperial, now thoroughly alarmed, sat bolt upright.

'You are going back to the ballet!' it accused.

'Maybe,' said Doura. She essayed an arabesque.

'It wobble,' said the Imperial critically.

'Wait,' said Doura. She essayed again.

'Pas mal,' said the Imperial impressed.

'In three weeks,' said Doura, 'I shall be all right. Not as good as I was,' she conceded, 'but good enough for Covent Garden. There,' she said fondly, 'they do not notice what they see. They see only what they remember—and that is me at twenty-three.'

'I remember you too, my darling,' said the Imperial.

'This is no time for sentiment,' said Doura Dourakova. 'And-one-and-two-and-three-and-four.' . . .

And so it was decided that Doura Dourakova should appear at Stroganoff's opening at Covent Garden. Needless to say this decision was not achieved without

Tears,

Tantrums,

Tumult,

Pleadings (The Imperial Beard)

Shruggings off.

Soyez raisonables (Stroganoff)

Shruggings off.

'You will be 'orrible' (Arenskaya)

Tears.

'Look at your be'ind.' (Arenskaya.)

Blows.

'Oh, good show.' (Lord Streatham.)

'But it's marked presto!' (The Conductor.)

'It shall be marked 'ow I wish it.'

'I don't want to be rude, but how can I be kind?' (Caryl Haskell-Beaumont.)

An appeasement of small scheques. (Nevajno.)

A scrutiny of contracts followed by a great deal of self-reproach. (The Webster One.)

Backer Trouble.

Indignation. (The Mothers.)

Rumours. (Everybody.)

And a dogged series of heart attacks.

But in the end the divine Dourakova had got her way, as she had done for half a century, and passed on to her next battlepoint—what should she wear?

'Impossible,' said Doura and tore up the design that was Nevajno's conception of a suitable costume for the Black Marketeer's mother. (The Life Force.) 'I will not dance in a black sack even if it is transparent.'

'There can be no other costume,' said Nevajno loftily and it was evidence of the state into which Doura had got him that he was reduced to explaining what hitherto he had airily stated. 'Life,' he explained, 'it is dark and therefore the sack it must be black.'

'Entendu,' said Stroganoff approvingly.

'But,' said Nevajno, 'life is not the end and therefore one must be able to see through the sack.' He looked at Stroganoff.

'Entendu,' said Stroganoff with a shade less assurance.

'I will wear,' said Dourakova firmly, 'my costume for Esmeralda—the one I wear the night our Poor Dead Tzar he did not come. I go to the dressmaker at once to show her.'

Tears!

Storms.

Hysterics.

The walk out.

The rush back again.

And so on.

But if Dourakova was difficult about the dresses how much more difficult was the dressmaker. For one thing she wanted to be paid, just as if she did not know that a backer never put money in the bank till the profits (or the bailiffs) came in, and that flattering money out of a backer before that was like flattering a fang out of a serpent.

'Seven hundred pounds?' said the Backer. 'Sure—sure! I'll send you round a cheque. Have another drink?'

'When?' asked Stroganoff anxiously.

'Right now,' said the Backer. 'Same again,' he told the barmaid.

'No, no,' said Stroganoff. 'I do not mean the little drink. I mean the little cheque.'

'What a one you are,' said the Backer largely. 'How much did you say it was?'

'Seven hundred pounds,' said Stroganoff, 'and fifteen shillings,' he added, feeling he might as well try for the rapidly mounting drink bill.

'Well, well,' said the Backer. He raised his glass. 'Cheers.'

They were in that snug little pub on the side of the theatre, where the orchestra was always to be found when it wasn't playing and sometimes when it should be. Here also came the back-stage personnel, front of the house personnel and their buddies. Here the really difficult business was transacted while the telephone calls piled up on the switchboard.

'The cheers,' said Stroganoff, playing his fish. 'To our season. Soon you will make much money.'

'Can't afford to make money,' said the Backer alarmed. 'Same again,' he snapped.

'Soon,' said Stroganoff, 'seven hundred pounds and fifteen shillings will be like the butterfly bite.'

'Seven hundred pounds!' said the Backer brooding. 'That's a lot of money for a few fal-lals.'

'Not when the fal-lals fit,' said Stroganoff. 'And 'ow they fit.' He kissed his fingers, deeming it politic at the moment to refrain from mentioning the innumerable sessions with the dressmaker or the screaming fits that invariably accompanied each one of them.

The Backer had another drink.

'Oh well,' he said. He pulled out his cheque book and looked thoughtfully at the single cheque left in it. 'Seven hundred pounds, you said?'

'And fifteen shillings,' said Stroganoff. He passed his fountain pen.

The little Baskova came in.

'And where have you been, darling?' asked the Backer. He put down the pen. 'Have a drink,' he offered.

'Darling doesn't feel like drinkies,' said the little Baskova, eyeing the cheque book. 'She's got to go down to the Bank to draw her last twenty pounds to keep her poor old mother in the country—far,' she underlined, 'away in the country.'

'Can't have the old lady knocking about in town,' said the Backer quickly. He picked up the pen, scribbled, and tore. 'There you are, darling,' he said.

'But my seven 'undred,' mourned Stroganoff.

'And fifteen shillings,' said the Backer. 'Sorry old boy, but I haven't got a cheque left. I'll send it round first thing to-morrow. No,' he remembered, 'to-morrow's Saturday. I'll send it on Tuesday when we get back from Brighton. Remember to remind me.'

He tucked his arm under the little Baskova's. The little Baskova winked at Stroganoff. They went.

'That will be thirty-seven shillings,' said the barmaid.

'I send you round the cheque,' said Stroganoff.
He vanished.

'Have another slice of cake,' said the Duchess hospitably.
'Enchanté,' said Stroganoff. He munched. 'You make it yourself?' he asked.
The Duchess beamed and nodded.
'With the dried egg?' pursued Stroganoff, interested.
'Certainly not,' said the Duchess. 'The eggs come from my farm.'
The farm fascinated Stroganoff. 'Ah—the little chickens in the backyard,' he said. 'You count them before they hatch—no?' He wagged a jovial finger at her.
'You're a nice one to talk,' said the Duchess indulgently. 'If you didn't count your chickens too soon you wouldn't be in this mess.'
'But I am in no mess,' said Stroganoff largely. He munched away. 'The little difficulties—yes, but what businessman has not the little difficulties to-day?'
'True,' said the Duchess.
'I lunch at the Savoy,' said Stroganoff, 'where my Relations Public he has the tick,' he explained, 'and the table on my left say "Ai!" and the table on my right say "Oi!" and in front there is the table that bury its head in its hands and behind me there is the head waiter, who is cross because there has just come in one whom he does not know and he cannot turn him away as he would like for there are many tables empty and the shareholders considered must be. But though all the others are black in the face,' said Stroganoff, 'I alone am gay.' He reached for another slice of cake.
'Steady,' said the Duchess.

'Poof,' said Stroganoff. 'You send to your backyard for a chicken and you make another. Yes,' he resumed, 'I am gay for though maybe I am in the salade I am not yet in the soup.'

'It sounds a pretty good soup to me,' said the Duchess.

'Aha!' said Stroganoff, 'you do not know a soup when you see one.'

The two old friends looked at one another. They laughed together as old friends do. They had been old friends for a fortnight now, and their friendship, like all the best friendships, was founded on enmity.

There is a phase in everyone's life where, whichever way they turn, they keep bumping into the same not very desirable acquaintance. This phase had hit Stroganoff and the Duchess of Dumpshire immediately following their first encounter at Fortnum and Mason's. The Duchess had only to accept an invitation to dinner to find Stroganoff, not only present, but sitting beside her. Stroganoff had only to arrive late at a theatre to have to 'pardon' his way past the Duchess' stall. Even when both were tempted to buy strawberries off a barrow they had to pick the same barrow and there was only one basket left at that. Stroganoff won this battle mainly by allowing himself to be charged plenty while the Duchess was haggling. In the restaurants, in the shops, on street refuges hemmed in by crawling traffic, the meetings continued. And when Stroganoff, one rainy morning, sprinted after and eventually caught a taxi, it was only to find the Duchess confidently entering by the opposite door.

Could any friendship start off under better auspices? Particularly as a common foe was presented forthwith in the shape of the taxi driver, who refused to take either of them.

'Don't you know a ruddy glove round a flag when you see it?' he demanded.

'Park Crescent,' said Stroganoff majestically. 'She pay you double,' he promised.

'Urcher,' said the driver. But he ground his gears and started off.

'I will do nothing of the kind,' said the Duchess. I don't believe in tipping.'

Stroganoff looked at her sadly. 'But you are a child,' he said. 'The innocent baby . . .'

The baby failed to annihilate him.

'The little bribe,' said Stroganoff, 'how could the good Russian exist without it. And that remind me,' he side-tracked. 'You come to my opening and I arrange for your picture in your Tatler.'

'I've had my picture in my Tatler,' said the Duchess of Dumpshire coldly.

'Me too,' boasted Stroganoff. 'The full page in the evening dress with the carnation. But not in colour,' he complained.

They rattled up Portland Place.

'They are good these old houses,' said Stroganoff approvingly. 'I have a flat here one season,' he informed her, 'but I do not pay the rent so they kick me out.'

'Indeed,' said the Duchess. 'How very disagreeable.'

'Oh, I have often been the kick-out,' said Stroganoff airily. 'The successful impresario he cannot avoid this. One day,' he suggested, 'you shall cook me the little dinner and I shall tell how many times my address it change quickly, sometimes,' said the bald-headed Sheherazade, 'with the furniture and sometimes without. The first time,' he remembered fondly, 'it was in the spring in St. Petersburg in the year that they did not kill Rasputin. The snow was falling and I am on my way to pawn my overcoat for soon it will be summer . . .'

The taxi pulled up in Park Crescent.

'We're here,' said the Duchess. She sounded slightly disappointed.

'I tell you the rest the next time we do the bump-in,' promised Stroganoff. 'My Bank,' he directed the driver. 'The interview embarrassing,' he confided to the Duchess.

The Duchess made a concession to curiosity. 'Would you care to come in for a cup of tea?'

'Enchanté,' said Stroganoff. He leapt out of the cab. 'We have the Russian tea, please—yes? See I have the lemon.' He pulled one out of his pocket.

They went upstairs and while Stroganoff showed her how tea should be brewed and lamented the absence of a samovar, the Duchess tried in vain to bring back the conversation to a further instalment of the pawned overcoat.

This was the first of the little tea parties. It was followed by others. Soon Stroganoff had got into the habit of popping in and pouring out his troubles, never stopping to listen in return when the Duchess told him hers. Stroganoff liked the Duchess, which calls for no comment, for Stroganoff liked everybody, but the Duchess who liked nobody, began to like Stroganoff which was so unusual that she wouldn't even admit it to herself. And every time Stroganoff took tea with the Duchess he invited her to his opening just as hopefully as though it were a brand new idea and every time the Duchess would refuse, sometimes kindly, sometimes briskly, but at all times very firmly. Just as she was waiting to do at this moment.

'Yes, my darling,' said Stroganoff, 'when it comes to the soup you are the child. I would not even be in the salade if you would but allow me to tell the press you come to my opening to-morrow night. Look,' he tempted, 'I permit that you do not arrive till the second ballet.'

'Stroganoff,' said the Duchess, 'I shall not be there. Have you decided what Doura will wear yet?' she asked with relish.

'It is decided that she shall wear the costume by Nevajno,' said Stroganoff. 'This is agreed by all except Doura. She persist that she will wear the Maryinski tu-tu that she carry out of Russia when she escape. But me,' he announced, 'I have the little plan for Doura.'

'Tell me,' wheedled the Duchess. 'I won't split,' she promised.

'But it is simple,' said Stroganoff. 'I give her faithful dresser the little bribe to burn the bodice with her iron at the last minute so that Doura she must wear the Nevajno costume or,' he spread his hands, 'nothing. And Doura is modest. Sometimes,' he remembered.

'But will the costumes be ready?' asked the Duchess.

'They will be ready if they are paid,' said Stroganoff. 'A little late maybe, but they will be ready. I have much trouble with the dressmaker,' he confided. 'For many weeks now she ask the little advance but always for the Rich One it is the long week-end. And when he returns himself he has no cheque book, and before he get it—poof—it is the long week-end again.

'You should let me get at the rich one,' said the Duchess. 'I'd give him a piece of my mind.'

'Non,' said Stroganoff. 'It is not the mind the Rich One wants. He is not reasonable, this Rich One,' he complained. 'The little shilly-shally from the business man, that one expects. That he leaves me always to pay for his lunch, that is natural. That he upset the Webster One and insult the press, that too is normal. But that he do not pay anything yet that—that——' emotion overcame him, 'that is too much.'

'And not enough,' said the Duchess.

'Promises, promises,' said Stroganoff. 'Always the to-morrow. But to-morrow there is no cheque in the book, and then it is the long week-end. And meantime I have to pay from my pocket and in my pocket there is nothing. You lend me the half-crown for the taxi?' he demanded.

'Certainly not,' said the Duchess.

'Then how I get to Covent Garden?' asked Stroganoff hurt.

'Walk,' said the Duchess.

'Walk!' Stroganoff tasted the idea. 'No,' he rejected it, 'for I am in the hurry enormous. The dress rehearsal start two hours ago which mean,' he looked at his watch, 'that in twenty minutes now, it will commence.'

'Well, what can happen at a dress rehearsal?' asked the Duchess.

What can happen at a dress rehearsal?

As Stroganoff came hurrying in at the stage door a piece of scenery came trundling out. It was wearing a bowler hat at each end and two pairs of boots.

'Look out, guv'nor,' said both ends simultaneously.

Dazed, Stroganoff pinned himself against the wall and watched it trundle its way past him into the street. Dazed, he watched it trundled into a van. Dazed, he watched the driver climb into his seat.

'Why you stand there like a fish?' Arenskaya came screaming at him. 'Do you not see it is our décor?'

'Of what use?' said Stroganoff heavily. 'They do us the
Or Else.'

The van moved off.

'Why you not run like a rabbit?' screamed Arenskaya.

'And what I do when I catch it?' demanded Stroganoff.

But he ran. Together they lolloped down Floral Street.

A stubborn tomato-barrow and a shouting potato-lorry
came into conflict. Swerving round the vocal deadlock the
van shook out a canvas lamp-post and lumbered on its way.
The cursing Arenskaya shook her fist after the van. The
panting Stroganoff salvaged the lamp-post.

'It is well painted,' he said critically, and held it up to the
tomato-barrow for approval. The barrow went on shouting.
'Maybe,' said Stroganoff, 'with this and the curtains black
we borrow from the Webster One it will pass.'

'It will pass well enough,' said Arenskaya, who had
fought violently against Nevajno's conception of a Square
in Soho from the moment she had seen it.

'And it will also be less expensive,' said Stroganoff, 'for
now we do not pay the Alec Johnston. That,' he said
happily, 'will teach him never again to write the letter that
begin—"unless".'

'His paintings he can keep,' said Arenskaya.

Arms linked, perfectly happy, and waving the lamp-post
at the autograph-hunters, they wandered on to the stage
and a fresh crisis.

The dressmaker was there. She was brandishing a
pair of scissors and screaming her head off. In front of
her, being screamed at, stood Nevajno. He was screaming
back.

'Sssh,' said Stroganoff to Arenskaya. 'My children dispute
themselves.' He started to tiptoe off.

The quarrellers sighted him, stopped screaming and pounced.

'Vladimir,' said Nevajno majestically, 'you instruct this woman,' he pointed at the tensed dressmaker, 'to stitch as I have designed or,' he considered, 'Else.'

'Unless I am paid at once,' said the dressmaker, small but livid, 'I shall stitch no more.'

'Poof,' said Stroganoff from force of habit.

It failed to soothe.

'This,' said the dressmaker, 'is the last straw. You talk me into this crazy job just when Cecil was on his knees to me to do Charley's Aunt. Every time I start on one of your lousy designs you scrap it. I work all day, I don't sleep at night, I drive my girls mad, my husband's getting fed up and I can't say I blame him, you've been promising to pay me every day for a month and never have and never will and what's more,' she swung round on Arenskaya, 'you owe me three and fourpence for cigarettes.'

'Now she throw the Cut Navy in our face,' said Arenskaya, as one who has suffered much and in silence. 'After all we do for her.'

'I'll tell you what I'll do for you,' said the dressmaker ominously. 'Are you going to pay me or are you not.'

'To-morrow,' said Stroganoff quickly.

'That settles it,' said the dressmaker. She clicked her scissors. 'Now,' she announced, 'I am going to slash every costume I can lay my hands on.'

'Starting with this one?' said the magically materialized Doura Dourakova sweetly. She held out a transparent sack.

'No!' yelped Nevajno in agony.

'Yes,' screamed the dressmaker. She fell on it, and with Doura helpfully turning the material, slashed it to pieces with far more skill than she had shown in putting it together.

'My sack,' mourned Nevajno. 'Fabricated special to see—through in Scheco-Shlovakia.' He turned tragically to Doura. 'What you wear now?'

'My Maryinski tu-tu,' said Doura. She hipped her way off.

The dressmaker was prowling the stage looking for more ribbons to rip, with the corps-de-ballet scuttling in all directions at her approach. Arenskaya made after her with the lamp-post. Nevajno lay on the floor and screamed. Stroganoff ran round in circles, flapping his hands and imploring everyone to keep as calm as he was. The Conductor did a crossword puzzle.

A stomach stood up in the stalls. It belonged to the Backer.

'What's all this?' he demanded. 'I thought it was going to be a dress rehearsal. I've brought the missus.' He pointed to a larger, grimmer stomach sitting beside him and frowning like anything.

'Villain,' screamed Stroganoff leaping to the footlights. He remembered himself and stretched out his arms.

'You are here at last, my friend,' he said. 'I welcome you. You have enjoyed your long week-end?'

'Sssh,' said the Backer urgently.

'What's that?' said the larger stomach.

'Back in a moment, darling,' said the Backer. He sidled out of the stalls and on to the stage.

Stroganoff rushed at him.

'The scheque,' he panted. 'And if there are no more scheques in the book I tear your stomach out.'

'And I help,' declared Arenskaya. She extended her hands and clawed her fingers.

'Easy, easy,' said the backer, backing. 'I'll send you round a cheque in the morning.'

'In the morning?' said Stroganoff fiercely. 'And in the morning it is the long week-end again—yes?'

'Sssh,' said the Backer apprehensively. For the Missus had extricated herself from her stall and was advancing towards them from the wings.

'Oho!' said Arenskaya, taking her in. 'The long week-end at Brighton?' she asked loudly. 'You enjoy yourself?'

'It was business,' said the Backer equally loudly and much more quickly. 'Urgent business. How much money did you say you wanted?' He pulled out a wad of notes.

Stroganoff began to calculate.

'Here's a hundred,' said the Backer generously. He peeled off a note. 'Cash,' he pointed out.

'The little Baskova?' asked Arenskaya. 'She enjoy Brighton too?'

'And two hundred more,' said the Backer in a hurry.

'She is a kind girl—the little Baskova,' said Stroganoff, catching on. 'Very loving,' he explained.

The Missus had reached the Backer's elbow.

'Very fond of bed,' said Arenskaya. 'N'est ce pas?'

'Here—take the lot,' said the Backer. He thrust the wad on Stroganoff.

'Ah bon,' said Stroganoff. He stowed it away.

'Wally,' said the Missus.

'Just a moment, my love,' said the Backer. 'Stroganoff, when do I see the accounts?'

'In the mornings,' said Stroganoff blandly. 'After the long week-ends.'

He trotted happily off with sundry creditors hurrying hungrily after him.

'Wally!' said the Missus.

The little Baskova came trotting happily on.

'Daddy, daddy!' she cried with appealing excitement. 'I'm dancing the Prelude. Isn't it lovely? And I owe it all to you!'

'Ssh,' said the Backer violently.

'Wally!' said the Missus.

Only just in time the little Baskova pulled back a hug.

'Er,' said the Backer, 'Miss Baskova—this is my wife.'

'Oh,' said the little Baskova. Disconcerted she giggled. Then fled.

'Wally!' said the Missus.

If only the ground would open and swallow him up!

It did.

'Trap door working okay, Joe?' asked the first stage hand conscientiously.

'Working fine, Bill,' said the second stage hand.

'Wally!' wailed the Missus, peering down.

The little Baskova couldn't resist it. She came back and pushed.

'*The most interesting feature of Aurora's Wedding was the length of the interval that preceded it. The clapping before the lowered curtain was as loud as any during the evening.*'

. . . 'My children,' said Stroganoff sorrowfully above the cannonade of clapping that percolated through the crimson tabs on to the Covent Garden curtain, 'would you do this thing to your papoushka?'

'We would,' said the Corps-de-ballet in seven different languages.

It had been a crowded day, starting with a Big Disappointment. The wad bludgeoned out of the Rich One did not on inspection turn out to consist entirely of hundred-pound notes. Most of them were fivers. There was enough to pay the hotel and lodging bills and to take away the scissors from the dressmaker, but the orchestra and the company were still unpaid and definitely brooding over it. So was the Webster One.

'Have in me the confidence,' urged Stroganoff in his dressing gown. 'Yesterday the rich one escape me. But to-day I pin him down by the ears.'

The early birding Webster One looked unconvinced.

'That is what you told me a month ago, Mr. Stroganoff,' he said. 'We are not accustomed to doing business this way at The Garden.'

'You are not?' said Stroganoff astonished. 'My friend, you should be in the Ballet Business.'

'I am in the Ballet Business,' said the Webster One coldly.

'Mais non,' said Stroganoff indulgently. 'Covent Garden —it is not the ballet. There everything is the grease——' The Webster One eyebrowed him, 'Wheel,' he finished. 'My friend, to be in the Ballet Business it is not enough to sit in your Opera House and choose which company you will permit to appear. That at last you have chosen me, I am grateful, and though maybe we have the little troubles, soon they will be over and you will see that you have chosen wisely.'

'You think so?' said the Webster One politely.

'But do not imagine because of this that you are in the Ballet Business,' said Stroganoff. 'No, my friend. To be in the Ballet Business you must go with it to Biarritz, to Barcelona, and to one night stands all over America. You must go with not enough good dancers and every day some

must leave you and others refuse to join. You must go
without money and you must get it from backers with little
Baskovas. And no matter if you have played to nothing
you must always see to it that your company has eaten once
that day at least. You have breakfasted—no?' he remembered.

'I wouldn't mind a cup of coffee,' said the Webster One.

'I order the breakfast delicious,' said Stroganoff. He rang
a bell. Nothing happened. It had ceased to happen in this
particular room over a fortnight ago when Stroganoff's
former lavish tips had trickled down to promises of free seats.

'Yes, my friend,' continued Stroganoff. 'You are not in
the Ballet Business at Covent Garden, you are in,' he sought
for the word, 'the cushion,' he found.

There was a knock at the door. It was not the breakfast.
It was a page boy with a registered letter. It began:

To One Lamp-post . . .
Dear Sir,
  Unless . . .

'Coffee!' said the Webster One sternly to the page boy.

A difficult day indeed. First the Webster One before
breakfast. Then the wheedle for the breakfast itself. This
triumphantly achieved through the influence of the hungry
Webster One, the wheedle at the laundry to boil a shirt in
time for opening. Then the telephone to the Rich One to
find that he had left his house but had not yet arrived at his
office, and the passage evasive with the rich one's wife, who
ask many questions to which only the wife of a backer
would not know the answer. The arrival at Covent Garden
to find Arenskaya screaming, the daughter of Doura in tears,
and the costumes not yet arrived. Pure routine but not very

soothing. The little plan with Arenskaya to lure away the Webster One and the quick sidle past his secretary to use his telephone for fifty-seven first-night wires, and the wheedle at the laundry. The borrow of a taxi fare from the stage doorkeeper with the heart of gold. The careful pricings of every bloom on the presentation bouquets assembled by Fortnum and Mason, not for reasons of economy but to avoid jealousies between the comparing eyes of the smiling recipients. The awful moment when the Goddess at Fortnum's brought the bill. The suspense while she telephoned Lord Streatham. The wild relief when the old school, though clearly shaken even at this distance, didn't let him down. The joyous ride to the Rich One's office. The two-hour wait, whiled away with wheedles at the laundry, during which the Rich One would be back at any moment. His simultaneous return and rush out, with his over-shoulder promise to bring the money round himself that afternoon. Repeating this assurance to everyone who bearded during the afternoon. A series of telephone calls to the be-back-at-any-moment Backer, ending in a fair cop only to learn that there was no time now, old man, but I'll be round before the show starts—rely on me. Telling this to the Webster One. Warding off the orchestra. Warding off well-wishing old acquaintances hoping for free seats. Warding off the Mamoushkas. Warding off, by mistake, the laundry. A sudden unexpected command for the Royal Box on behalf of the Duchess of Dumpshire, involving the dislodging of a Shipping Line, with difficulty persuaded to attend only this morning by Lord Streatham. The dislodging of two minor peers to find a box for the Shipping Line. The moving of two M.Ps to find stalls for the peers. And so on till Stroganoff and Streatham would have to stand at the back of

the circle. Finding by this time that it was six o'clock and
the audience arriving already. Borrowing a shirt and taxi
fare from the Webster One. The arrival of the Balleto-
Medico. (It was not Doura who was having a heart attack
this time, but Doura's daughter.) The arrival of the Shipping
Line. The arrival of the two Peers. The arrival of the M.Ps.
The re-arrival of the Balleto-Medico. (It was not Doura's
daughter who was having the heart attack—it was the
Shipping Line.) No arrival of the Backer. The arrival of the
entire corps-de-ballet already in their tulle mists demanding
to be paid or Else. The crisis postponed with the little
promises from Stroganoff and the little screamings from
Arenskaya. The arrival of the Duchess of Dumpshire, all
smiles and old lace and expecting to be thanked for it. Her
Progress past the Shipping Line. The rapid reappearance of
the Balleto-Medico.

The curtain ten minutes overdue to rise. Routine.

No appearance of the Backer. Also, more or less routine.

Les Sylphides.

Black Market.

No Backer.

'My children,' Stroganoff was saying above the per-
colating impatience of the waiting house, 'is this the way
to treat your papoushka? Dance for me this one ballet and
then you shall be paid.'

'You promised to pay us after Sylphides,' said the thin
girl. She glared.

'And after Black Market,' said the Fat Girl. She giggled.

'And now I promise to pay you after Aurore,' said
Stroganoff. 'What more you want?'

'We want it now,' said the corps-de-ballet in seven
languages.

The clapping on the other side of the curtain grew louder.

'So,' said Stroganoff, a wounded Cæsar looking at Brutus, 'you hold me the pistol and stab me in the back. Ah! If my company were but Russian this thing could not happen.' He glared at the one English girl in the company.

'Swolotz!' said the English girl.

The clapping swelled.

'Come, come, my children,' said Stroganoff. 'Do not ruin us all. You dance for me Aurore like the little angels, and,' he tried a new approach, 'I get Arenskaya to let you off class to-morrow.'

The corps-de-ballet looked tempted. But the thin girl stood firm.

'We want our money,' she said. 'Now.'

'When the Rich One comes,' said Stroganoff. 'This he has promise me.'

The Webster One came striding across the stage. He managed not to run. He handed Stroganoff an evening paper. The headline read:

CITY MAN ARRESTED AT AIRPORT.

'Why you worry me with this now?' asked Stroganoff crossly.

'Read on,' said the Webster One.

Stroganoff looked at the picture of a smiling, cigar-smoking face.

'Oh, Mon Dieu!' he said, 'it is the Rich One.' He concentrated. 'Aie! Aie!' he groaned.

'What 'as happen,' asked Arenskaya, rushing in to scream.

'It is the end,' said Stroganoff heavily. 'Max Intrator has schanged schmall scheque for the Rich One.'

'Mon Dieu!' Nicolas Nevajno, who up to now had been hanging around waiting for the quarrel to subside so that attention might be diverted to congratulations for his Black Market, had paled and sat down heavily on Aurora's throne. 'Intrator has schanged me schmall scheque too.' He stood up. 'I shall perish in a dungeon,' he announced.

The applause was swelled with whistles.

'Calm yourself, Nicolas,' said the Stroganoff. 'It do not count with the English police when your scheque it bounce.'

The thin girl drew herself up. 'Well,' she said, 'that settles it. We don't dance.'

'Oh yes, you do,' snapped a voice from the wings. And it had the authority of centuries behind it.

The Duchess of Dumpshire, awful in old lace, stalked on to the stage.

'Stroganoff,' said the Duchess, 'what is keeping the curtain down?'

'It is the strike sit-down,' said Stroganoff. 'They will not dance because they think I cannot pay them.'

'And can you?' asked the Duchess.

'No,' said Stroganoff.

'Well, I can,' said the Duchess.

The girls looked at the old lace. It carried conviction.

'But,' said the Duchess, 'if the curtain doesn't rise within two minutes, I won't.'

And while Stroganoff was still embracing the Duchess in the wings, it did.

Caryl Haskell-Beaumont crumpled up the evening paper and flung it viciously into the gutter.

'Cut me to hell,' she complained.

Pop Went the Weasel

'YOUR health,' said the stranger with the pint. He lowered most of it. 'All the same,' he said, 'it was a bloody lucky winner.'

'That's what you think, said Ginger. 'That's what you all thought.' He gazed through a haze of alcohol and happiness at the fringe of imbibing but slightly envious faces. 'Same again all round, Gwennie,' he ordered, 'and a ginger wine for yourself.' He puffed his cigar. 'I been waiting for that dog to run in its own class to put my shirt on it. And I did,' he reminded himself blissfully.

A murmur, not altogether of approval, ran through the public bar of the Lord Nelson. The stranger whistled a little tune. It was 'Pop goes the Weasel.'

'How come you had a shirt to put on, Ginger?' asked the Skipper of the Skylark.

'On a Thursday night what's more!' said the man from the turnstile on the pier.

'Oh, I had it,' said Ginger without much mirth. 'I had it all right. And now,' he produced a fortune out of his pocket, 'I got all these shirts to take with me on my holiday the day after to-morrow.' He waved seventeen pounds in the air.

'Going away?' asked the stranger.

'Now, I am,' said Ginger. 'To Blackpool,' he swanked.

'Sally's there with her Ma. Won't they be surprised to see me?' he gloated.

'I'm from Blackpool myself,' said the stranger. 'Blackpool's all right if you've got a bit of money in your pocket.'

'How come you had a bit of money in your pocket on a Thursday, Ginger?' asked an Irishman in an overall.

'You're always broke by Tuesday,' said the deck-chair ticket collector.

'You borrowed five bob off me yesterday,' said the driver of the trolley that ran up and down the pier.

'Here's your five bob,' said Ginger, rather pink. He flung it at him.

The trolley driver turned an even bricker red than before.

'Steady, Ginger,' said Turnstiles. 'Can't you take a joke?'

Ginger couldn't.

'What's it got to do with you where I get my money from?' he shouted. 'You're glad enough to drink it, aren't you?'

'Well, I'm not drinking any more of it,' said the Irishman, 'and that's straight.' He poured his beer on to the floor.

'And don't you come to me for any more five bobs till Friday,' said the trolley driver, 'or you'll get something else.'

'Come outside,' said Ginger, 'and I'll give it you now.'

'You and who else,' said the driver. He crouched.

'Boys, boys,' said Gwennie. 'What's come over you. You back a dog and you get above yourself,' she accused.

'Why can't they leave me alone,' demanded Ginger passionately. 'What's it got to do with them where I get my money?'

'Why, chum,' said the stranger gently, 'anyone'd think you'd been robbing the till.

*   *   *   *   *

The till.

It stood on the counter of the staff canteen at the top end of the pier. It was two quid short. But it didn't bank till Saturday. And here came Ginger, bright and early on this Friday morning, to put them back before the manageress got there.

His temper was all right again. His mood was sunny. He might have pinched two quid yesterday (though you couldn't really call it pinching—borrowing was the right word), but he was an honest man and he was on his way to prove it. Anyone could borrow a couple of quid, couldn't they? But not everybody could pay it back so quickly. Led all the way! Never in doubt for a moment!

'Hey, Mister!'

A small boy was thumping petulantly on the glass case of a toy crane. 'I put in my penny, Mister,' he complained, 'but it won't work.'

'Let's have a look, son,' said Ginger. He ran a professional eye over the crane, specially designed not to pick up any of the more expensive Wonder Gifts littered under it. 'Have it right in a jiffy,' he diagnosed.

For getting things right in a jiffy was Ginger's job on the pier at Kilburn Sands, which contained a great deal of apparatus needing to be put right during the season. Including the till in the staff canteen. That's how he'd got at it. Enough to tempt a millionaire. Though you couldn't really call it pinching—not to put on Merry Matador— Borrowing was the word.

'Hey, Mister!' said the small boy.

Ginger went to work with a screwdriver.

'Here you are, sonny,' he said a jiffy later. 'It's all right now.' He went off whistling.

'Hey, Mister,' wailed the small boy after him, 'I ain't caught a Wonder Gift!' . . .

The canteen was as empty as a Sunday school. There was a nice cheerful sound of bustling behind the partition and the homey smell of toast and kippers hung about the place. Ginger remembered that he hadn't waited for a bite of breakfast that morning, but the important thing was to get the two quid back. It had to be timed right between the moment that Daise opened up and went into the kitchen and before the manageress arrived to bustle around like an overboiling tea-kettle with never an eye off the till. And he had timed it right too. Good old Dora—unpunctual as clockwork. You could always rely on her being two minutes late. Another jiffy and he'd be an honest man.

Holding a spanner in his hand, just for the look of the thing, he converged on the till and rang it open. One shake of a cow's tail and he could look himself in the face again. But before the tail had time to whisk a whistle penetrated the canteen.

'Hello, chum,' said the stranger from Blackpool, 'robbing the till again?' He sat down at a table and finished his whistle.

'Pop goes the Weasel.'

Ginger looked at him with loathing. This man was a menace.

'If you must know,' he said, 'I'm the mechanic on this pier and I'm testing it—see!' He clanged the till shut and moved away, the sixteen half crowns still a weight in his pocket.

'What you doing in this canteen, anyway?' he demanded. 'It's staff.'

E

'So'm I, chum,' said the Menace. 'I'm on the staff and I want some breakfast.' He banged on the table.

Daise put a reproachful head round the corner. 'What's your 'urry,' she said. She put it back.

'Have a bite with me, chum,' invited the Menace. 'If we ever get it. I'm the Welfare Officer,' he explained.

' 'Oos welfare?' demanded Ginger bristling.

'Yours,' said the Menace largely. 'Hers.' He jerked his thumb. 'Everybody's. Welfare Officer to the Pier—that's me.' He put his thumbs in his armpits and twiddled. 'My job's to see that you're all happy.'

'Oh is it?' said Ginger.

'So if you got any complaints, chum, out with them,' said the Menace. He banged the table. 'Where the heck's that breakfast?' he bawled.

Daise stuck her head round. 'What'll you have?' she asked. She put it back before they could answer.

'Joining me?' asked the Menace.

'I got work to do,' said Ginger. He gathered up his tools.

'Be seeing you,' said the Menace in no way snubbed.

'Guess so,' said Ginger.

He wandered out.

Just round the corner stood the penny-in-slot machines, ancient peepholes to Edwardian high jinks that had taken many a penny in the days when a penny was a penny. Well, maybe it was worth it in them days, thought Ginger, as he gazed at the voluminously draped bathing belles ticking over before him. But that Floozie on the third postcard was a peach. He put in another of the penny-shaped discs that were part of his equipment and had her tick over in front of him again. He wondered what she'd look like in a bathing costume. A real one with no middle. Not as nice as Sal, you bet. He wondered if anybody had got off with Sal at Blackpool. Well, he'd be there himself to put a stop to it to-morrow.

He put a disc in 'A Night in Paris.' Very tame, he thought, for Paris.

What the Butler Saw! He could have taken his grandmother with him.

An enormous hand walloped him on the back.

'Hello, chum,' said the Menace. He smelt of kippers. 'Let's have a peep.'

'Put in your penny,' said Ginger frigidly.

The Menace laughed heartily. 'You got a nice job, you have. See it all for nothing. I'd try to hang on to that job if I were you, chum. Pop goes the weasel.'

'What d'you mean!' said Ginger.

'Just my fun,' said the Menace. 'Only people do lose jobs you know.' He became businesslike. 'Where's the pier-master's cabin?'

'Round there.' Ginger pointed with relief.

'Ah well,' said the Menace. 'Be seeing you.'

'Guess so,' said Ginger.

'Be good,' said the Menace.

'What d'you mean?' said Ginger.

'Don't go robbing any more tills.' The Menace wagged a playful finger and strode off whistling.

Blooming busybody, thought Ginger. He picked up his tools and hurried back to the canteen.

He knew it. The blasted place was full and Dora was boiling about all over it. Not that that made her take her eyes off the till. Still she had called him in to put it right yesterday, hadn't she? So why shouldn't he take a look to see that it was in order to-day? Put a bold face on it.

'Hello, Dora,' he called. 'Just going to check up on that till of yours.'

'Now don't you worry your head about that, ducks,' said Dora, bustling right up to it. 'It's working a treat.' She demonstrated. 'See!' she said. 'I reckon it won't give any more trouble the rest of the season. Now just you sit down and have a nice cup of tea on the house. Daise,' she yelled, 'bring two nice cups of tea—*with*,' she emphasised.

So Ginger had a nice cup of tea *With*, right under the till, and watched Dora get up to ring it open every time someone paid a bill and never take her eyes off it once to give a chap a chance to slide sixteen half-crowns back into the bloody drawer.

'Works a treat,' she kept on gloating.

Why couldn't she get a telegram to say her old mum was dying? If she did she'd take the bloody till with her. Not a chance now to put the two quid back till after the lunch hour rush when Dora steamed out to do a bit of shopping.

'Well, Dora,' he said. 'Got to be off now. Yours ain't the only thing that goes wrong on this pier, you know.'

'It works a treat,' said Dora, absently.

So Ginger went about his work, whiling away the time till Dora went off to do her bit of shopping so that he could get the money back. It wasn't going to be as safe as it would have been this morning—but for the Menace. He'd have been an honest man again by now but for the Menace. Looked the whole world in the face and owed not any till. Took an educated man to make a joke like that. He'd have gone a long way if he could have gone on to a Secondary.

He wouldn't have been just a pier mechanic having to
borrow two quid to put on a dog. He might have been—
well—a welfare officer. And then maybe Sal's old woman
wouldn't snap his head off quite so free. So he wasn't good
enough for Sal, wasn't he? Well, he wasn't, but what right
had her old woman to keep saying so. Still she'd pipe a
different tune when he turned up at Blackpool with seventeen quid and his new shirt.

The Piermaster went parading by in a salty glory of
braid, beard, and nautical gait that would have deceived
anyone except a sailor. He bowed to a deck chair. He fine
day'd a promenader. He failed to nod to Ginger. Ginger
scowled after him. He might have been a Piermaster if he'd
gone on to a Secondary and a darn sight better one.

'Hi, Ginger!' The Brown Linen Jacket that presided over
the pin-table parlour beckoned to him. 'Been waiting for
you all morning. Come and have a look at number
seven.'

'Okay,' said Ginger. 'What's wrong this time?'

Number seven was a skating rink in which if your ball
was truly aimed bells rang, lights blazed, and a ballerina
went spinning all over the place. Only the bells wouldn't
ring, the lights wouldn't blaze, the ballerina stood on one
skate and looked like remaining there for keeps and the
small boy who hadn't got a Wondergift was howling the
place down.

'Have this right in a jiffy,' said Ginger. He bent over the
machine.

The small boy stopped howling. He had confidence in
Ginger's jiffies. He watched enthralled as Ginger opened up
the jammed machine and scooped the pennies out of the
overflowing bank.

'Hello, chum,' said a hated voice. 'At it again?'

Ginger turned with his hands full of coppers. The Menace popped the weasel and grinned.

'I'd keep an eye on him if I were you,' he counselled the Brown Linen Jacket with professional jocularity.

'What d'you mean?' said Ginger hotly. 'You take that back.'

But the Menace, well pleased with his wit, had inserted a penny in the aerodrome next door and was assisting, not very ably, a Spitfire in its jerky take-off.

'Who's your friend?' asked the Brown Linen Jacket.

'Welfare Officer,' said Ginger shortly.

'Who's welfare?' demanded the Brown Linen Jacket.

Ginger felt better. 'His bloody own,' he said.

What with one job and another the time went by, and pretty soon it was going on for half-past two and Dora was steaming off to do her bit of shopping. Trying not to walk too quickly Ginger hared off to the canteen. There would still be a few people about the place, but he'd have to take the chance. If he put a bold face on it, marched right up to the till, rang open the drawer, clanged it about a bit and put in the sixteen half-crowns while he was clanging, it should be all right. He was the pier mechanic, wasn't he? And a mechanic had a right to make sure he'd done his job proper, hadn't he?

But even as his hand fumbled at the door of the canteen a whistle came round the corner. It hit Ginger right in his courage. Before his brain had time to protest his feet had landed him straight through Gipsy Rosa's curtains and bang in front of Gipsy Rosa.

'Hello, Ginger,' wheezed Gipsy Rosa, half-way between

a husky dove and a dulcet foghorn. 'Come to cross my palm
with silver?'

The Weasel, hanging about outside, was plainly audible.
'Might as well,' said Ginger at bay. 'Mind you,' he
defended himself, 'I don't believe a word of it.'

But when Gipsy Rosa got down to it and produced a
dark stranger to beware of, who boded him no good and
who was always crossing his path, Ginger's scepticism was
visibly shaken.

'Like me to look in the crystal, dearie,' said Gipsy Rosa
encouraged by her grip on her audience. 'Half a crown it is,
dearie, but seeing as it's you, I'll make it two bob.'

The Weasel had gone, but Ginger stayed on fascinated.

'Okay,' he said. 'Mind you, I don't believe a word of it.'

Gipsy Rosa got down to it again. 'It's clouding over,' she
crooned. 'It's getting clearer. I see a lot of people at a race
track—no,' said Gipsy Rosa, who had her sources of
information, 'it's a dog track. I see a dog—a wonderful dog.
You got a lot of money on that dog . . .'

'Never mind the past,' said Ginger quickly. 'Tell us the
future.'

Gipsy Rosa shot him a shrewd look. The cunning old
brain got there or as near there as makes no difference. She
huddled closer to the crystal.

'I see a room,' she improvised. 'It's very small and very
dark, and,' a flashing, grimy finger pointed dramatically
upwards, 'there's bars across the window.'

'I don't believe it,' said Ginger.

Gipsy Rosa ignored him. 'There's a man sitting in that
room with his head in his hands—wait a minute—I'll try
and see the colour of his hair. Why, Ginger!' she said,
'what have you been doing?'

'Me—nothing!' said Ginger. He pulled himself together. 'I don't believe a word of it,' he said defiantly.

He shook Gipsy Rosa off and blinked his way into the daylight.

Two bob gone! Might have got himself a nice yellow tie for two bob.

Furious with himself he strode into the canteen. Anger had replaced fear.

'Hello, chum,' said the Menace from the table by the till. 'Been expecting you.'

Fear came back. But he wasn't going to show it.

'Hello,' said Ginger. He sat right down beside him.

'Something told me you'd be coming here,' said the Menace.

'Must have been the tea leaves in your cup,' said Ginger. He meant it as a joke, but it came out a bit tart.

'How many times have I bumped into you this morning?' asked the Menace happily. 'Five or is it six? Ah well! It's all in a day's work.'

Daise came up. 'Everything's off,' she said. She plonked down a cup of tea and a slice of very sandy cake in front of him and went off.

The Menace lit a pipe. Blimey, thought Ginger, won't he ever go?

'You know,' said the Menace, 'I like it here at Kilburn Sands. I think I'm going to like this job. Everybody's friendly. Everybody,' he took his pipe out, 'except you.'

'Something's eating you, Ginger. You're not happy—are you? What's on your mind, Ginger?'

'Murder,' said Ginger, not without truth.

The Menace laughed professionally. 'Come, come,' he

said, 'it can't be as bad as all that. Out with it, chum. Let's
see if I can do anything to help.'

'It'd be a help if you got out of here,' said Ginger with
complete truth.

'That's not the spirit,' said the Menace full of professional
kindly reproach. But he got up. No good forcing a confidence. 'Well, you'll always find me about the place if you
want me. Be seeing you.' He walked out.

Ah!

Ginger sprang up. But almost immediately he sat down
again. The Menace had come back.

'Forgot my pipe,' he beamed forgiveness. 'Be seeing you.'
He went off whistling.

This time Ginger decided to wait a full minute for him
not to come back again. Before it was up Dora had steamed
in boiling over with parcels.

'Hello, Ginger,' she waved. 'Give us a hand with the
parcels, Daise,' she bawled. 'It works a treat,' she assured.

The pier was filling up nicely when Ginger emerged
dispirited from the canteen with his sixteen pieces of silver
still dragging down his pocket. Kilburn Sands was more of
a family resort than Blackpool, or Hoy, and now a steady
stream of them came clicking through the turnstiles to
settle into deck-chairs, listen to the band, laugh at the
pierrots, eat ice-cream and pay no attention to 'Now mind
and don't go away too far, Willie!' and 'Marleen, come
away from that there railing and stop asking the fishing
gentleman why he ain't caught nothing—he don't like little
girls.' Glare.

Ginger marched among the families, not looking at the
pink-faced girls, not even noticing their pretty bosoms. No

hope now of getting that blasted money back till half-past five when the canteen closed for an hour. And a mighty slim chance then. He'd have to slip it back between the time Dora steamed off and Daise locked up. Nice girl, Daise, when she wasn't being nasty.

Ginger mooched past the bandstand. They were playing Richard Tauber while red-faced mommas beat time and red-faced poppas read their morning papers and red-faced kids wouldn't sit still. He peered into the pin-table saloon. The skating ballerina had broken down again. He moved quickly on before they could spot him. He was in no mood for work.

The trolley car clanged past him on its way to the pier-head. The driver elaborately cut Ginger dead. The manner of the return of the five-shilling loan was still rankling.

Who cares, thought Ginger uneasily. He leant over the rail of the Dodge'em cars and watched the Berts and the Gerts bumping into each other and screaming. Lucky Berts—they were allowed to be honest.

A strong sense of injustice pervaded Ginger's soul. What sort of a world was it when you couldn't put money back you'd borrowed. Borrowed, he told himself firmly.

A majestic presence tapped him on the shoulder.

'I want a word with you in my office,' said the Piermaster sternly.

Cripes!

With terror in his heart Ginger followed the nautical gait along the pier. Dora must have found out! But how did they know it was him? And if he said it wasn't could they prove it was?

The Piermaster led the way into his cabin and closed the door.

'Well?' said Ginger. He swallowed.

'The lock's gone,' said the Piermaster. 'See what you can do about it when you get a minute.'

He gaited out.

Ginger was so relieved that he suddenly felt fond of the door. It should have the best lock he could get from the store—to-morrow. Meanwhile, he'd put a bolt on, when he got round to it. Funny how he didn't feel like work to-day. Funny how having something on your mind sapped your energy. A bit of a rest where no one could get at him—that wouldn't be bad.

Ginger went off in search of it.

'Come to my garden of love,' invited the fat pink lady with the pom-poms. 'Come! Come! Come!' she invited each time on a higher note. Then she bowed and sat down. It was perhaps as well that the rest of the pierrot troupe were there to help to swell the applause.

And now the comedian went at it with a will, working his not very funny number with his eyebrows, his elbows, his hands and a very bright sports jacket; trotting out his corny jokes as proudly as though he had made them up himself. He was playing the part of a tripper to Kilburn Sands and what happened to him was no inducement to anyone else to trip there. But it went well with the trippers.

Ginger too leant back in his deck-chair and roared. He had forgotten to look at his wrist-watch, he had forgotten that he was lying low until between Dora and Daisy time, he had even forgotten the sixteen half crowns in his pocket. An ideal audience, Ginger.

Came Number seven, A Night in Paris, and a holiday-maker in suede shoes (the baritone) put a penny in a peep-

show and turned a handle that didn't. So he summoned the
mechanic (the comedian). The comedian came on in an
overall and dropped a spanner on the baritone's toe. The
baritone hopped. The comedian peered into the peepshow.
He went on peering long after he had mended it.

'Let's have a peep?' pleaded the baritone. 'It's my penny,'
he argued.

'And it's my machine,' said the mechanic.

Ginger laughed like a drain.

The comedian went on peeping and turning.

'She's taking her petticoat off now,' he announced. He
mimicked her action with one hand and held back the
baritone with the other.

There was another drain behind Ginger, gurgling,
guggling and very nearly splashing. And then, instead of
clapping it whistled and Ginger shot out of his deck-chair
like a startled rabbit and hared for the exit.

'Something's worrying that fellow,' mused the Menace.
He determined to seek out Ginger and break down his sales
resistance and look after his welfare whether he liked it or
not.

'Oh, we do like to be beside the seaside,' sang the pierrots.

Meanwhile Ginger was out in the clear, with his troubles
full on him again and ten minutes to go before Dora did.
Where could he hide? Just his luck to be pounced on to do a
job now.

'Hi, Ginger!'

He knew it!

The fussiest man on the pier came clucking up. 'Where
you been?' he demanded. 'Been looking for you all afternoon. We've broken down. Turning away good money

and you nowhere in sight. I'll report you, that's what I'll do. Come along. Hurry up. What you waiting for?'

There followed a frenzied ten minutes with Ginger in Fairyland working against time. One of the mining dwarfs couldn't wield his pick—it was no worse than that, but the fussiest man on the pier seemed convinced that any seven-year-old seeing him on strike would instantly demand his money back. Ginger's attempts to leave it till morning were deluged in a spate of words, all of them reproachful and presently he was lying on his stomach under the dwarf with the fussiest man fussing over him and Dora already wriggling her toes into her wedge heels.

'There you are,' said Ginger thankfully. He scrambled up.

The dwarf swung his pick twice and lost interest. But not the fussiest man on the pier.

'Try a bit of oil,' he advised.

'I'll get the oil can,' said Ginger. He scrammed.

Past the half-hour! Ginger ran towards the canteen. He ran right past Daise talking with the girl that sold the Kewpie dolls, discussing Rita Hayworth. Then he stopped running. What was the good. He mooched round to the back of the locked canteen. Maybe Daise had left a window open.

She hadn't.

Ginger mooched round to the front again. An hour to go before the canteen would reopen for the evening staff. Might as well have his bit of supper early on the pier. And maybe there'd be a chance to get at the till and put the sixteen half crowns back.

It *was* borrowing!

'Got the oil?' The fussiest man on the pier pounced.

'It's after my hours,' said Ginger sulkily.

A whistle came floating round the corner.

The mechanic underwent a change of heart. 'Come on,' he urged, and for the first time in his career entered willingly into Fairyland where he oiled not only the dwarf but the Fairy Queen and her entire realm and even went as far as to touch up the mushrooms with a lick of red paint. But all this took only twenty-five minutes and then the fussiest man on the pier, unused to not urging willing workers on, lost his impetus and got bored.

So Ginger found himself on the pier again with thirty-five minutes to wait and the trippers going home for supper and the pier emptying fast, but with the Menace presumably still on it. With despondent gait Ginger betook himself to the jetty where a solitary fisherman was not catching any fish and sat down to watch him not doing it. And he sat there, with his shoulders hunched, his heart as heavy as his pockets and his fag continually going out, thinking what a day it had been, the Menace loomed larger and larger in it until the whole day seemed made of the Menace with his hearty laugh and his sinister whistle. Always on to him like a detective. Maybe that's what he was. A detective.

What did he know?

The thought drove Ginger from the bench to the side of the jetty. He looked down at the peaceful waves lapping their way towards Kilburn Sands. A grey-blue restful grave. Ginger for pluck! Suppose he jumped in and drowned himself? Suppose he drowned the Menace? That was more like it! Get at that fat throat, stifle the whistle, and throw him in. Lovely splash he'd make. And then nothing but a lot of pretty ripples and he could put his money back in peace.

Ginger gazed at the waters imagining the fat face of the Menace floating under them. He could see it.

By God! He *could* see it.

He turned. It was right there beside him.

'Hello, chum,' said the Menace. 'Enjoying yourself?'

Ginger gazed at the fat throat that he had just had his hands on. He restrained himself.

'I was,' he said.

'Thought you'd be gone by now,' said the Menace. 'Isn't it after hours?'

'What if it is?' snarled Ginger. 'Can't I enjoy the sea air— same as anyone else.'

'If you got a clear conscience, you can,' said the Menace. He breathed luxuriously.

That did it.

'Leave me alone,' screamed Ginger suddenly. 'Leave me alone, I tell you. Leave me alone . . .'

The fisherman looked up.

'Hush,' he said severely.

He went back to not catching fish.

'Take it easy, chum,' said the Menace soothingly. 'I'm not aiming to upset you.'

'Well, you are upsetting me,' said Ginger. 'So get out of my way and stay out.'

'Why, chum,' said the Menace gently, 'what harm am I doing you?'

'Harm!' Ginger quivered. 'You're making me a murderer—that's all.'

He strode off.

The Menace looked after him. Something mighty odd there. Better keep an eye on him, he decided.

There was no chance to get at the till when the canteen opened. Dora had got there first

To his own surprise Ginger made a hearty meal of boiled cod and boiled cabbage—and all to the accompaniment of the ringing of the till.

'It goes a treat,' said Dora, nodding at him encouragingly.

And as Ginger's hunger grew less his anger grew greater, and he thought he was like a small boy with his nose glued to a sweet-shop window. So near . . . So near . . .

And then suddenly the shop window melted.

Dora had slid off the stool by the till, on which she had seemed so inexorably perched, and was putting on her hat. Dora, who had never been known to leave the canteen between six and closing time, when she preceded Daise by some five minutes before the all-off whistle, which incidently would be Ginger's last chance to put the money back before the totalling up first thing to-morrow.

Ginger thought quickly. He got there. What he had to do was to keep Daise up to her eyes in the kitchen. He beckoned urgently. Daise slithered up.

'That'll be one and twopence,' she said.

'Bring me a pair of kippers,' said Ginger, 'and while you're at it I'd fancy some chips as well, fried as only you can fry 'em.'

'No chips,' said Daise.

'Oh, come on,' said Ginger. 'Be a sport, Daise.'

In face of so much flattery Daise weakened.

'I'll see,' she said. She slithered off.

Dora had got her hat on to her satisfaction. She came and stood in front of Ginger smirking all over her face.

'How d'you like it?' she asked.

It was a horror, even without the price ticket still hanging on it, boiling over with ostrich feathers and steaming with tulle.

'Suits you a treat,' said Ginger glibly. He should worry what it looked like as long as she went out in it.

'Good,' said Dora. 'Glad you like it.' She took it off, hung it up, and sat down at the till.

Daise was bearing down on him, carrying the chips, as only she could cook them, which even at this distance could be seen to be greasy.

'Oh hell,' said Ginger.

He slammed out.

'Hi, Ginger!' wailed Daise hurt, 'I got your chips.'

'Hi, Ginger!' shrilled Dora, 'come back. You've forgotten to pay.'

Right outside the canteen, grinning all over his stupid face and looking as though he'd been planted there was the Menace, and if he wasn't whistling it was only because he was eating Kilburn Rock.

'Hello, chum,' he said with his mouth full, 'still enjoying the sea air?'

'Can't enjoy anything with you around,' glowered Ginger. 'I'm packing up for the day and I'm off to Blackpool to-morrow, and with any luck you'll have the sack before I get back—you nosey Parker, you!'

After which gracious farewell he pulled his cap over his eyes and stalked majestically off.

The majestic stalk lasted quite a few steps. But round the corner, out of sight of the canteen, it dwindled to a dejected shuffle. Now why the hell had he told the Menace he was going off the pier? Hadn't he got to stay on it till the canteen closed?

Ginger leant over a rail and gazed at the Dodge'em cars, now fuller than ever with Berts and Gerts and other anonymous screamers. On impulse he put down a savage sixpence. He'd bump the guts out of them.

Ginger was class with a Dodge'em. Ask Sal! The accumulated venom of the day found expression in electrifying bursts of speed and fiendish bumps. You couldn't knock over a Dodge'em with another Dodge'em, but, by God, you could try. And you could make 'em squeal all right. There was one Bert in a nice yellow tie, who didn't half fancy himself with a Dodge'em and his Gert didn't half fancy him too. Ginger concentrated on him. Five minutes grim assault and the Bert in the nice yellow tie was telling his Gert that she looked as though she had one of her headaches coming on. Ginger scowled with satisfaction as they departed. Now who would he take on next?

He found another Bert and Gert. He dealt with them faithfully. He went on to deal with others. Battered and shaken the Berts and Gerts began to thin out in search of other amusements. One way and another Ginger was costing the proprietor quite a bit of money. But Ginger himself was beginning to feel a lot better.

There was a group of Dodge'ems in the centre clustering together as though for mutual protection. Ginger took up a position and made a deliberate charge into them. Swivelling and bumping he fought his way through and ended up with a glorious head-on with the Dodge'em in the centre. He grinned triumphantly at the driver. The driver grinned back.

'Hello, chum,' said the Menace. 'Not gone yet.'

'I'm going now,' said Ginger whitely. He climbed out.

'That'll be five bob,' said the proprietor.

'Be your age,' said Ginger. He vaulted over the rail and became merged with the promenaders round the bandstand.

The band was playing Tauber, the Mommas were beating time, the fathers were reading their evening papers, and the kids wouldn't sit still. In the distance Ginger spotted the Menace emerging from the Dodge'ems.

The trolley train was about to leave for the foot of the pier. Ginger dived into the covered car and closed the door.

It was a lovely evening. Mommas and kids piled themselves into the open coaches to breathe the sea air, lose their balloons, and squeal at one another. Nobody wanted to sit in the dusty, closed coach. Nobody disturbed Ginger.

It was good to be alone. The sudden peace of isolation, the steady trundling of the wheels, the muffled screams of the children all acted as a potent lullaby. And as the sky grew darker and the pier lights flickered on, Ginger, riding up and down, up and down, passed from fear and strain into sleep.

And the Menace, with his suspicions still very vague but definitely growing, walked about the pier, whistling away and acquainting himself with the night staff. And looking for Ginger everywhere. But it never occurred to him to look inside the closed trolley car.

A whistle from the pier-head woke Ginger. He stood there blinking. Was it the All Ashore? No, thank God, it was only the Visitors Off.

As the long-drawn whistle died away, Ginger sprang out of the trolley. The trolley driver, taking off his overall, blinked, remembered he wasn't speaking, and looked the other way. So much the better.

Ginger sprinted towards the canteen. Or rather he would have sprinted but the remorseless tide of home-going Alfies, Mums and Minnies slowed him down to shoving.

Loathing the lot of them Ginger arrived at the bandstand.
The going was easier now. Only a few entwined couples to
dodge. Dora would be gone by now and Daise locking up
at any moment.

'Steady, chum!' warned a butted stomach reproachfully.
But it wasn't the Menace.

'Why don't you look where you're going?' demanded
the stomach's bridling wife.

But Ginger was. The lights were still on in the canteen
and he was making for them like a one-way moth.

Funny, it looked as though there were quite a few people
in the canteen.

Ginger was right. There were quite a few people in the
canteen. The whole night staff. They were being harangued
by the Welfare Officer, who had mounted the counter, and
in a great many words, glib with repetition, was telling
them over and over again that all he wanted was their
happiness.

'So, chums,' he was saying, 'if you got any complaints, if
you don't feel you've been done right by, if you don't think
you got a square deal, if you imagine someone's being unfair
to you, or—to cut a long story short—you got any complaints, don't bottle it up and take it out on your nearest
and dearest. You come and have it out with me and I'll see
to it that its put before the proper authorities. And by You,'
he drew up his resources for the final effort, 'I mean You.'

And he pointed his arm straight at Ginger, who had come
shooting in and who now shot out again.

Still here. Hanging around. Not gone yet, thought the
Menace. Fishy. But there were other things on his mind
just now.

'And so, chums,' he resumed, 'if you ain't happy in your work, if you can't come to terms with your job, if you're the right man in the wrong place, if you're a round peg in a square hole, and if . . .'

There was a tug at his sleeve.

'It's getting late,' boiled Dora.

Not knowing where he was taking himself and caring less, Ginger found himself outside the piermaster's cabin. He'd never got round to putting that bolt on the door.

What a thing to think of with prison staring him in the face!

How long would they give him? Whatever it was Ma would be bound to tell Sal she'd always told her he was no good. Would Sal wait for him? Like Trevor Howard?

The door was opening. Ginger dodged. The piermaster came out. His personality had suffered a sad diminishment. He was just an ordinary man in a tweed coat, a pull-on cap, and not an inch of gold braid anywhere. He closed the door carefully, tut-tutted at the broken lock, and went forlornly down the pier.

An idea came to Ginger. He slipped into the cabin. He made for the piermaster's uniform, meticulously hung on a privately-purchased hanger and felt through the pockets. He pulled out the keys of the pier and everything on it.

Including the key of the canteen.

Saved! All he had to do was to wait till they'd all gone home, put the money back, put the keys back, and go home himself.

Ginger broke into a whistle. 'It's a lovely day to-morrow, to-morrow is a lovely day.'

To-morrow was Blackpool. To-morrow was Sal.

Better wait a few minutes to make certain they'd all gone. And while he was waiting he might as well put a bolt on that door.

Blast it, he hadn't got a bolt!

Ginger read the Kilburn Sands Gazette. It wasn't very enthralling. He wandered round the cabin looking at the photographs of earlier piermasters and not a pin-up girl among the lot. Even the blonde above the calender had all her clothes on.

Friday the 13th.
'Honesty is the best Policy.'

That's what they thought!

After all, he'd only borrowed it.

The pier whistle blew three times. All Off.

Ginger gave them three everlasting minutes while he re-read the small ads, and then, very cautiously, he opened the door just as Dora steamed by, oblivious, with, in her wake, the Menace, hands in pockets, whistling and nothing like so oblivious.

Ginger slammed the door shut and shrank into a corner. As an afterthought he turned the light out.

Had the Menace spotted him? Was he hanging about outside? Was that his bulk or just the shadows? Was he to stay cooped up here all night to go to prison in the morning? Or was there some way out?

'Are they all off?' the Menace asked Turnstiles.

'If they ain't that's their funeral,' said Turnstiles. 'I'm locking up.'

'Ginger gone yet?' asked the Menace.

'Ginger? He goes off at five,' said Turnstiles. 'Try the local,' he suggested.

Fishy!

The Menace moved away and leant over the railings.

'Locking up,' said Turnstiles sharply.

'Go right ahead, chum,' said the Menace. 'I'm going to hang around a bit.'

'Well, mind your trousers when you're climbing over,' said Turnstiles. 'Good night.'

'Good night, chum,' said the Menace.

And now there was nothing but the Menace and Ginger and the dark pier and the quickly darkening night.

The Menace filled his pipe.

Still here. Not gone yet. Hanging around, brooded the Menace, carefully working it out in triplicate. He's up to something, that lad.

Conscientiously plodding along this train of thought the Menace put two and two together and produced a triumphant five. Why had Ginger said he was going off when he wasn't? Why had he stayed on after everyone had gone? Why had he been so touchy in the pub last night—just like a man being asked questions he doesn't like answering. Where had he got the money to put on Merry Matador?

He'd caught Ginger at the till that morning. He'd caught him emptying the pin-table bank. Ginger was always hanging around money. That's what he'd stayed behind for. Money. He was going to rob the till!

But Ginger had backed a winner. What of it? Easy come, easy go. There'd be other winners at the dogs to-morrow.

Ginger was going to rob the till. The Menace felt as certain of it as he had ever felt about anything in his life. And here they were alone together on the dark pier.

The Menace felt in his pockets for his torch, not so much to light the way as to give him something to cling on to.

A nice start to a new job!

Very slowly, very softly, he made his way up the pier, shooting his light into dark corners in case Ginger was lurking in one of them. He was never a man for physical violence, but, if it came to a scrap, well—Ginger was smaller than him.

And so the Menace came to the canteen. It was dark and deserted. The Menace pressed himself against the wall and lurked. He thought of the Daring Dexters. It cheered him up a bit.

A shadow detached itself from the shadows. The Menace caught his breath. It came striding firmly towards the canteen, produced a bunch of keys, and began trying them in the keyhole. He waited till a key had gone in. Then he switched his torch full on a white yachting cap and a lot of gold braid.

God Almighty—it was the piermaster.

Now what do you do if you catch the piermaster opening up his own property after hours? Awkward. Instead of asking him what he's doing you've got to tell him what you're doing. Tricky.

'Er,' said the Menace.

'Cripes!' said the Piermaster. He abandoned the keys in the lock and ran.

The Menace gave chase. Fishy, he was thinking.

Ginger knew the pier like the back of his hand. But the Menace had right on his side. And while Ginger dodged frantically from here to there, the Menace rumbled steadily on and wouldn't be shaken off.

The Dodge'ems! Ginger vaulted over the rails and crouched behind a car. The Menace came lumbering up and ran his torch over the floor. He lit up a white yachting cap. A fine way for a piermaster to behave. But of course it wasn't the piermaster. It was Ginger all right, Ginger disguising himself to rob the till. Awkward though, if it wasn't.

The Menace dismissed the thought and levered himself over the railings to chase the white cap now climbing out on the other side.

But he couldn't scramble over railings as quickly as Ginger and by the time he had scrambled over both, Ginger was nowhere in sight. But he'd find him if it took all night.

Conscientiously the Menace went plodding along the pier. He shone his torch into the dark secrets of Gipsy Rosa's booth. He examined the Kewpie doll kiosk. He explored the bandstand and even looked under it. He rattled the locked doors of the Pierrot's hut. He made his way through Fairyland on all fours, crawling laboriously along the passages. And so, inevitably, he came to the Moving Picture Gallery in which Ginger had hidden himself.

Meanwhile Ginger, skulking among the penny-in-slot entertainments, felt boredom getting the upper hand of terror. He wandered from machine to machine—the static Tower of London in which a slotted penny would produce a jerky execution. The equally still magician with a telescope who, suitably stimulated, would clap it to his eye and deliver a printed character card at you. The motionless House on Fire. Where was the Menace now? Had he got fed up and gone home? Maybe the uniform had fooled him. Maybe he'd tripped over an anchor cable and broken his blasted neck. Ginger gave himself up to an orgy of wishful thinking.

A bell rang. The gates of the fire station opened. The fire engine clanged out and jerked its way to the house on fire. Up flew a window, a lady in lingerie flung out her arms and swooned. Up went the ladder, up went the gallant fireman, steadily and unemotionally, up went the lady over his back, down came the fireman steadily and unemotionally.

Quite automatically Ginger had dropped in a metal disc.

'Enjoying yourself, chum!' said a soft voice at his elbow. Ginger butted it in the stomach and ran.

Cursing the Menace disentangled himself from the Tower of London and resumed the chase. That was the trouble with the Menace. He couldn't resist an effect. If he'd grabbed he'd have caught Ginger instead of a lot of broken glass.

Outside Ginger made straight for the haunted house, slipped in by the back entrance and went into the bowels. The Menace would never think of that one.

The Menace didn't. But plodding conscientiously around he came on the piermaster's cap lying in front of the door. He pushed at the door. It opened. Throwing a careful light the Menace walked gingerly along the narrow musty-smelling passage that led into who knew what.

Crump—crump.

The floor was giving way under him!

He shone his torch on it. But it was only one of those effects that made the Gerts scream and cling closer to their Berts.

The Menace turned a corner and saw a swollen giant with a light charging at him. He ducked. So did the giant. It was nothing but a mirror.

'Phew!' said the Menace. But he wiped his brow, plodded on and came to a staircase. He began to plod down it.

Suddenly the whole place began to vibrate, and his feet to
slip from under him and there seemed no end to the steps.
And then the lights went on and he found he was going the
wrong way on a moving staircase. And at the bottom of it
was Ginger, who had switched on the machinery, and was
waiting for him with a very ugly look on his face.

The Menace stood still to consider. The staircase carried
him back to the top.

'Better come quietly,' he bawled, 'it'll be the worse for
you if you don't.'

But the echo of his own voice was all that answered him.
Ginger had disappeared again.

Presently the lights went out. But the haunted house
went on chugging and vibrating and generally making the
Menace's journey through it pretty horrible. The last straw
was when he clutched at what he thought was Ginger. It
turned out to be a screaming skeleton.

A further unpleasant surprise awaited him as he emerged.
Ginger was climbing over the pier railings, hand over hand,
lowering himself with tremendous care.

'Stop!' bawled the Menace.

'Not bloody likely,' bawled Ginger. Still very laboriously
he lowered himself out of sight. The Menace would keep
following him on top of the pier. Let's see if he had the guts
to follow him under it.

He had. Puffing, clinging, and testing every step of the
way, the Menace came swinging along the girders. The
slimmer Ginger felt very superior. He waited till the Menace
had puffed within a few feet, then quickly put twice the
girders between them.

'Come quietly,' urged the Menace resuming his slow
progress. 'It'll be the worse for you if you don't.'

'Sez you,' said Ginger. He swung off.

So did the Menace. Right off.

There was a splash.

That'll larn you, thought Ginger.

There was a silence.

Cripes! Supposing the Menace couldn't swim.

Quick as an eel Ginger was in after him. He grasped the coming-up Menace and dragged him, choking and spluttering, to the iron steps that led up to the jetty.

'Now what d'you want to get your clothes wet for,' said the Menace not at all in the manner of one whose life has just been saved. 'I can swim all right.'

'Oh, can you?' said Ginger.

'Nearly swam the Channel once,' boasted the Menace.

'Well, swim it again,' said Ginger.

He pushed him in.

Only one thought in Ginger's mind now. The till. He sprinted towards the canteen feeling furiously in his pockets for the keys. Cripes—must have fallen out. What the hell—he'd break a window. What was a broken window more or less with all the rest they got against him!

Dodging round to the back of the canteen, Ginger looked at Dora's beautifully-cleaned glass, sighed, shielded his head, and put his foot through it. Getting his body to crawl through the jagged glass uncut was a trickier business and just as he had managed it the canteen door opened, the lights went on, and there, dripping wet, stood the Menace.

'Why didn't you come in by the front, chum?' The Menace made his effect. 'I found these in the lock.' He jangled the bunch of keys.

Ginger socked him one. All the bitterness of the day went

into that sock and a bit of his longing for Sal and safety. The Menace sat down, very hard, on the floor, While he was rubbing his jaw, Ginger rang open the till, counted out sixteen half crowns and put them in.

'All right,' he said. 'I'll go quiet now.'

And he walked up to the Menace and held out his wrists for all the world as though the Menace had a pair of hand-cuffs.

*   *   *   *   *

'Another cup of tea,' said the Menace hospitably.

'Thanks,' said Ginger. 'Don't mind if I do.'

'*With?*' asked the Menace meaningly. He poured lavishly from Dora's private sugar ration.

It was half an hour later. They were sitting in their underwear with the gas-fire going and the piermaster's gold braid spread out in front of it. They had made themselves a pot of tea and Ginger had opened a tin of sardines.

It couldn't have been chummier.

'Well, I never in all my natural,' said the Menace not for the first time. 'Taking money out of a till is one thing, but going to all that trouble to put money in—well, I would never have believed it if I hadn't seen it with my own eyes.'

'You don't understand,' said Ginger. 'I'm an honest man.' He leant back glowing and relaxed. 'I never took the money in the first place. I only borrowed it. So I had to get it back—see?'

'Supposing the dog had lost?' asked the Menace.

'That dog couldn't lose,' said Ginger.

The Menace felt in his underwear for his pipe. It wasn't there. He took one of Ginger's gaspers and puffed.

'Well, chum,' he summed up, 'so you borrowed the money, and you put it back, and no one a penny the worse—

atchoo—excepting me. Now, chum, what would you be planning to do supposing—just suppose, mind you,' he wagged a podgy finger, 'I didn't report you.'

'You mean it?' said Ginger. His eyes glowed. 'I'd go to Blackpool with sixteen pounds in my pocket . . .'

'Fifteen,' corrected the Menace. 'You got to pay for Dora's window.'

'Fifteen,' agreed Ginger. 'And I'd get hold of Sal, and I'd give her ma the slip, and we'd go on the pier, Sal and me, and we'd listen to the pierrots and get a breath of sea air.'

'H'm,' said the Menace. 'What time d'you leave?'

'Mean it?' asked Ginger.

'Let it be a lesson to you,' said the Menace. 'You've stayed honest cos your dog came in. But remember,' he pointed a finger, 'it was a bloody lucky dog.'

'Lucky my aunt,' said Ginger. 'Merry Matador always wins in its own class. Bet you it wins again to-morrow.'

'Oh, it's running to-morrow, is it?' observed the Menace.

'You can put your shirt on it,' said Ginger. 'It'll trap in front and lead all the way—just as it did yesterday. Makes me almost sorry I shan't be there to see it. What's more, you ought to get seven to two for your money if you step in quick.'

The gas-fire spluttered and recovered itself.

'Now that's interesting,' said the Menace. He stroked his chin. 'Seven to two, you said. That's very interesting. Can't lose, you said.' He stroked it some more. 'Might have quite a bet to-morrow.'

His eyes travelled towards the till.

Ginger looked with him.

'Pop goes the Weasel,' he whistled.

Anything Goes at Christmas

ALL day long it had been snowing and Regent Street looked just like a Christmas card, only with hansom cabs instead of reindeer sledges.

It was the week before Christmas, 1907.

For the fifteenth time the Santa Claus outside the Regent Street Store blew on his fingers and envied the other Santa Claus who had the job inside the store outside the Lucky Dip. Not only was it warm in there, but there were the delighted cries of the little lucky dippers to tickle up the cockles of your heart.

All day long the doors of the Regent Street Stores had been swinging open to let in little eager boys and girls, as yet empty-handed but followed by full-pursed mammas, and to let out a stream of radiant little girls and boys, clutching parcels often as big as themselves, and followed by slightly less radiant mammas, trying to face the fact that they had spent more than they had expected and already formulating their answers ready for the moment when their husbands would discover it.

Inside the store all was the happiest confusion. Saucer-eyed children milled about, cooing and ooing, clutching their inexhaustible half-crown and wanting to buy the whole store with it, and here was a particularly spoilt customer crying because he couldn't. Helpful shop assistants shinned up step-ladders—took down, put back again, dug up from under, demonstrated—yes, they had something cheaper, or dearer, or unbreakable, or louder, or softer—and all with unvaried patience and no little head patted ('Against Our Rules') or clouted ('Instant Dismissal!')

Past the electric trains, whizzing round in circles, past the bright coloured forts guarded by lead soldiers, through the tangle of Snakes, Ladders, Ludo and Lotto, dodging the diabolos, hoops, and skipping ropes, and beyond the plasticine, painting boxes and picture books, stood the marvel of marvels—The Toy Theatre.

A miracle of gold and plush cardboard, flanked by boxes of clapping cardboard children, with a velvet curtain rolled up to show Little Red Riding Hood standing in the middle of a forest, and the Big Bad Wolf licking his chops round a portable cardboard tree; with a change of scene (Dick Whittington and his Cat), slotted into the back. All for forty-eight and eleven (carriage paid), with Aladdin and his Wonderful Lamp, three and six extra, including lamp.

'That's what I want,' said a small boy standing there with the look of a visionary in his eye. To make himself quite clear he pointed.

'Now, Noel, be sensible,' said his Mother. But the small boy shook his head.

'I want a featre,' he said firmly.

Besides the Toy Theatre, the Regent Street Stores had another special attraction. A display of talking wax dolls, straight from Paris, piping 'Pa-pa' and 'Ma-ma' in tugged harmony. A bobble of little girls, allowed by the assistants to tug for themselves, were beseeching their mothers to buy.

'Three gross and the lot will be gone by Christmas,' gloated the Senior Buyer, well pleased with his enterprise.

'In your place I'd have ordered double,' said the Junior Buyer. 'All little girls like dolls at Christmas. Look!' He pointed to the clamour of outstretched little hands.

'Eighteen and eleven is a lot of money for a doll,' said the Senior Buyer. He looked at a Mother, who was clearly saying the same thing.

'Not in Regent Street at Christmas,' said the Junior Buyer, as the Mother sighed, succumbed, and fumbled in her purse.

But eighteen and eleven was too much money for Hoxton—even at Christmas. Here the Paris doll that said 'Pa-pa' and 'Ma-ma' was priced at ten and sixpence, and even though it was the only one of its kind in Auntie Ringer's toyshop, the others being of the Dutch, or wooden, or rag variety, and though it had been on show for six weeks, and though it had been tugged and admired many times daily, it still ended up each evening not only unsold, but not even haggled over.

'Ten and sixpence! Three weeks' rent!'

The Paris Doll was Auntie Ringer's this year's Annual Extravagance. Last year it had been balloons filled with air that bobbled up against the ceiling of the shop and wore the new paint off. The year before it had been roller skates, and Auntie Ringer had felt personally responsible for every twisted ankle. So this year it was the pretty Paris doll that couldn't do anybody any harm, look at it as you might. And it only needed a Pa to have a bit of luck with a horse and one of the kiddies that thronged the little shop all day would be as pleased as Punch.

Auntie Ringer's Toy Shop had no Santa Claus, inside or out. But it had it's lucky dip (¼d.), it had its trains, hand-pulled on a bit of-string, it had its sweets, its marbles and its penny games of Ludo and Lotto, it had its clappers, its penny pistols, and its Japanese water-flowers. In fact, it had everything a child could need—including the well-merited clout on the head. And its customers cooed and ooed just as much as in any toyshop anywhere.

Only here the coos predominated.

'Coo,' said a curly head that reached just as high as the counter on which the Paris Doll had been prominently propped. 'Coo,' it repeated eloquently and stretched out a not-nearly-long-enough pair of arms as though to clasp the pink, cotton-backed, satiny splendour.

Auntie Ringer smiled indulgently. This customer had exactly twopence to spend, she could see it clutched in the outstretched hand—but no matter.

'Maudie shall show it to you, dearie,' she said. 'Maudie,' she called.

Maudie pushed aside her Educational Atlas. Oh dear, now she would have to start memorizing what it was Chile exported all over again.

'Maudie,' called Auntie Ringer, on her way back to preside over the Bran Tub (where she arrived just in time to prevent a small child throwing a fistful of bran over a slightly larger one). 'Maudie, come and show little Lucy the talking doll.'

'I knew it would be the doll,' thought Maudie, from the

wisdom of her eight Christmas weeks. But all the same she took it from its box and pulled gently at the strings.

'Pa-pa,' said the Doll. 'Ma-ma.'

'Coo,' said little Lucy. She extended her twopence.

'Here,' said Auntie Ringer, getting back from the Bran Tub just in time to thrust a rag doll, which ought to have brought in fivepence of anybody's money into little Lucy's arms. 'Here's a lovely dolly for you, ducky. Now say "thank you" and ask the policeman to see you across the road.'

'Fank you,' said little Lucy dutifully. She looked at her hand. 'I still got tuppence to spend,' she announced. She looked round the shop.

Another fivepence gone, thought Auntie Ringer. No wonder her books never balanced.

Auntie Ringer's was not just another dingy toyshop in a grimy street. All Hoxton knew Auntie Ringer's. She was the confidante of every child in the district, the counsellor of every mother and the avenging angel to all erring fathers, on whom she was apt to pounce outside the local public houses, crying 'Shame on you! And little Elsie needing new shoes!' Auntie Ringer ruled her shop as graciously and as firmly as Queen Alexandra ruled her household. She gave no credit but many a present, and if the shop was not always as solvent as it might be, well anybody could make money, but Auntie Ringer was making character.

And amid all this she brought up Maudie and the two boys and Baby to help her and help one another. And if she was sterner with them than with the other Hoxton children, it was for their own good in the long run.

'Maudie,' she called again. 'Come and show the Paris doll to Mrs. Jones' Lil.'

Once again the exports of Chile were left to rot in their own country while Maudie pulled the strings of the Paris doll she was getting to hate with all the fierceness of her eight Christmas seasons.

The Santa Claus outside the Regent Street Store was blowing on his fingers; the Santa Claus inside took off his beard, saw the frock-coated Floor Walker eyeing him balefully, and put it on again, a little sideways.

But closing time at Auntie Ringer's was at a much later hour. For one thing it kept the kids off the streets till the parents came out of the pubs to look after them.

But at ten o'clock the last little treble had been pushed out, the shutters had been closed and the Paris doll put in her box and covered up.

Auntie Ringer settled herself comfortably in the kitchen. She picked up the Educational Atlas.

'Now, Maudie,' she said, 'what are the exports of Chile?'

The Borough Council of Hoxton, though no Fairy God-mother, had the welfare of its population at heart. It had dotted several benches about the Borough, on which tired citizens could sit, while waiting for the horse-bus or just resting.

One of these benches had planted itself in the little alley-way that was the short cut to The Prince of Wales and the Board School. On it, just resting, sat an old tramp. He sat there every day and Maudie, on her way home from after-noon school, used to look out for him and smile and she passed. And the old tramp used to smile at Maudie and reflect that he might have had a nice little kid like that. He might have been in regular work . . . he shied away from the thought.

But this afternoon, Maudie did not smile. She trudged past, her plaits swinging, her head down, her goloshes kicking at the snow.

The old tramp missed something. Kids ought to be smiling at Christmas.

'What's up, matey?' he called. 'Someone been nasty?'

'Teacher's cross,' said Maudie. 'I didn't know know my exports from Chile.'

'Didn't do your homework, eh!' said the tramp shocked. 'Now you listen to me whot's old enough to be your father and learn it next time. Don't want to grow up and be h'ignorant, do you?'

'No,' said Maudie dubiously. She sat down beside him. 'I got more homework to-night,' she confided.

'Well, mind you do it proper,' he said.

'It's ever so difficult,' said Maudie. 'It's arithmetic.'

An early memory stirred in the tramp. 'I used to be good at arithmetic,' he mused. 'Knew all my multiplication tables by heart. Twelve twelves are . . .' He paused and grappled. 'Five fives are twenty-five,' he substituted.

Maudie opened her satchel and produced her exercise book.

'It's ever so difficult,' she said.

'Read it out,' said the tramp, interested. He prepared to concentrate.

'A and B,' read Maudie carefully, 'agree to help one another at Christmas, as all good neighbours should, to shovel away the snow in front of their houses. A can shovel snow twice as fast as B. But B,' she took a breath, 'can shovel snow twice as long as A . . .'

F

Shovelling snow! The tramp winced.

Excitement at the Regent Street Store. The huge stock of toys was dwindling so rapidly that full-pursed mammas, who had come determined to select judiciously and not be stampeded, were fast being reduced to grabbing what they could get.

At the special attraction stand the last of the Paris dolls was being handed over to a pair of outstretched little hands and all the other outstretched little hands were turning themselves into fists and rubbing their eyes.

'I wouldn't have your conscience for anything this Christmas,' said the Junior Buyer to the Senior Buyer.

Pandemonium at Auntie Ringer's. The Lucky Dip was besieged by customers, and try as she might Auntie Ringer was finding it impossible to prevent the lucky ones dipping twice for the price of one.

And in the middle of it one of the right sort of Pa's, who had picked one of the right sort of horses, came sheepishly in dragged along by Our Rosie.

'Merry Christmas to you, Auntie!' He put on an air to hide his bashful face. 'Show us what you've got!'

'Maudie,' called Auntie Ringer from her hot spot, 'come and show Mr. Jones the Paris Doll. And show it proper,' she exhorted.

Maudie stopped frowning dubiously over the tramp's solution, and came into the shop. She diagnosed Mr. Jones at a glance. She took down the doll. It might be the last time she would have to do it. She put her heart in it.

'Pretty,' said. Mr. Jones, sheepish again. ' 'Ow much?'

Maudie looked helplessly at Auntie Ringer. It wasn't the sort of news for a little girl to break. But Auntie Ringer was far too busy to look at Maudie. Maudie took a deep breath.

'Ten and sixpence,' she faltered.

'Cripes!' said the right sort of Pa.

He dragged Our howling Rosie out of the shop.

'Hello, nipper!' called the old tramp next afternoon. 'Was the answer all right?'

Maudie came to the bench and sat down, her legs dangling reflectively. She was a kind girl.

'Well,' she said, 'very nearly.'

The tramp braced himself. 'Got any more,' he asked heroically.

'No thank you,' said Maudie quickly. 'It's history to-night.'

'Ah,' said the tramp, relieved. Memory stirred in him again. 'Mind you learn them dates proper,' he cautioned. 'Alfred and the cakes,' he instanced.

'Well,' said Maudie, 'I got to be going.' She lowered herself off the bench.

The tramp felt an unaccustomed pang of loneliness.

'Stay a bit longer, matey,' he said.

'Can't,' said Maudie. 'Ma wants me in the shop. It's Christmas week,' she reminded him.

Kids oughtn't to work at Christmas thought the tramp indignantly. It wasn't right, that's what it wasn't. Kids ought to get presents at Christmas, not arithmetic that it took a full-grown man all his time to work out. Shovelling snow! Cor!

'Tell you what, matey,' he said. 'Meet me Christmas Day, same time, same place, and I'll have a little present for you— see if I don't.'

Now what had come over him to say that. A present. The tramp began to regret his promise. A moment later he didn't. For little Maudie was all red cheeks and shining eyes and clearly contemplating hugging the assorted miscellany collected from various washing lines and rag heaps that made up the tramp's working suit.

'I'll have a present for you,' he repeated confidently. 'See if I don't. Christmas Day, same time—same place.'

Maudie was gone. The tramp had time to brood on this thing into which he had so recklessly plunged. Presents cost money and money had to be earned. And earning meant work! And with his constitution, too!

The tramp settled down to decide what work he should do. He studied the possibilities. They'd take him on at the goods yard—if he was mug enough to offer! Santy Claus outside one of them West End Stores—all that standing about and him with varicose veins . . .

The tramp went on cogitating. But every job had an objection that spelt work. That's what came of doing arithmetic for a little nipper. Two men agree to shovel snow! What next!

It was Christmas Eve, and London was getting ready for the mood of benevolence, ecstasy and surfeit in which it proposed to spend the next two days. Streets were thronged with shoppers, cabs were hard to get, horse-buses were filled to overflowing, total strangers, laden and colliding, helped one another to pick up the fallen parcels and wished each other a Merry Christmas and even the beggars sported a sprig of holly and took time off to smile. And all against a background of roof-tops and chimney pots softened with snow.

London Harlequinade!

And here comes Pantaloon, trudging a residential street in Hackney, carrying a spade under his arm and muttering to himself. What can he be saying?

'Two men agree to shovel snow. Mugs like meself!'

He stops before a portico and surveys the snow on the steps with an expert's eye.

'Now, lidy, 'ave a 'eart,' he says. 'I never undertake to sweep the pavement too. Not for ninepence,' he pursues.

It was nearly seven o'clock on Christmas Eve and Auntie Ringer's shop was in a ferment. What was more, it would stay in a ferment till the early hours of the morning, for Auntie Ringer's did not close at all on Christmas Eve. The Ringer family was assembled in force to cope with the last-minute rush, and even Baby perched on a high stool was getting some early training in being allowed to lick the envelopes of the Surprise Packets ($\frac{1}{2}$d.).

In the kitchen was a huge heap of surplus oddments, the accumulations of the chaos of the preceding weeks. Coloured beads, isolated marbles, single lead soldiers, Jacks-in-the-boxes without lids, celluloid dolls with missing arms, trumpets that still sounded if you blew hard enough and masses and masses of Hundreds and Thousands. Every year the last-minute demand was enormous and every year the children sat in the kitchen, filling stockings almost as fast as Auntie Ringer could sell. And while the boys packed feverishly, Maudie sat sewing up the overflowing tops of the gauze stockings with scarlet wool.

So great was the crowd in the shop that the farthing dip had spilt all over the floor and was now closed down, the shelves were beginning to look empty, soon you would be able to count the marbles in the Four-a-penny bowl, and there wasn't an acid-drop in the place.

But the Paris Doll remained, propped on the counter, in unsold splendour.

'Pa-pa, Ma-ma!' said Auntie Ringer taking a moment off to scowl at it. 'A lot of good that's done you.'

The Regent Street Store, too, bore an unusually scavenged air. There were big gaps in the shelves, the display counters displayed less and less, the rocking-horses were thinned out, and even the billiard tables were being demonstrated.

'Anything goes at Christmas,' said the Senior Buyer.

Through the turmoil of coos and oos and 'is that all you've got left,' a little boy in a sailor suit came tugging a portly gentleman. He looked at neither the scarlet fire-engines, nor the clockwork automobiles. He knew exactly where he was going and what he would find when he got there.

'Look,' he said, 'the curtain goes up and down.' He demonstrated.

'So it does, Noel,' said the portly gentleman. 'Here—let me try.'

Time passed.

'I'll have two of these,' said the portly gentleman. 'You can send one to my office.'

The little boy in the sailor suit waited breathlessly while the assistant packed the parcel.

'Oh thank you, Uncle Cocky,' he breathed.

There was no Santa Claus outside the store to open the door of the cab for them as they emerged into the street. He was inside collecting his pay envelope.

Christmas in Regent Street was over for this year.

But Christmas was not yet over at Auntie Ringer's toy-shop. The customers were standing about waiting for their twopenny stockings. It was late at night and there was practically nothing else left—except the Paris Doll.

' 'Ow much longer 'ave I gotta wait?' asked a nodding rose in a rusty bonnet.

'You'll wait your turn, Mrs. Smithers,' said Auntie Ringer very firmly.

A stocking came through the hatch and was handed to a black woollen shawl. Mrs. Smithers moved up one.

And now a new customer stood in the doorway. His pockets were jingling, his heart was one large glow of self-satisfaction and virtue, and he towered there as though he owned the world.

Auntie Ringer gave him one look.

'Outside—you!' she said.

'Now, Ma,' said the tramp, hurt, 'your can't talk like that to a customer.' He looked round the shop and his eyes came to rest on the Paris Doll. ' 'Ow much?' he demanded.

'You're drunk!' said Auntie Ringer.

'Me!' said the tramp. 'I want a nice present for a nice little girl.' He pointed to the doll. ' 'Ow much?' he demanded again.

Auntie Ringer felt herself softening. Clearly a bad egg, but he wanted a present for a kid,

'Here,' she said and passed him an out-of-turn stocking, ignoring Mrs. Smithers' reproachful looks.

'Not good enough,' said the tramp, waving it away. 'I want the best you got. 'Ow much?' he pointed once more.

'Ten and sixpence,' said Auntie Ringer less harshly. 'So now forget it and take your stocking. Twopence,' she added, feeling that if he really had money she might as well get some of it before it went on beer.

But the tramp was emptying his pockets. Piles of pennies, threepenny bits, and here and there a larger piece of silver. He began to count laboriously while, with unbelieving eyes, Auntie Ringer counted with him.

'Nine and eightpence ha'pny,' totalled the tramp regretfully. He had earned it hard and it wasn't enough. That's what work did for you!

'Oh, get along with you,' said Auntie Ringer. She thrust the Paris Doll into his arms. 'It says "Pa-pa" and "Ma-ma," ' she added as an afterthought.

'Do it really,' said the tramp, impressed. 'She'll like that.' He stowed it away in his pocket, touched his cap, and began to shuffle off.

'Hey, you,' called Auntie Ringer after him.

Had she changed her mind? The tramp shuffled faster.

'It don't do to be broke at Christmas,' said Auntie Ringer. She gave him back a shilling.

Mrs. Smithers sniffed.

In the kitchen the boys' movements were getting slower and slower and Maudie was threading the scarlet wool practically in her sleep.

It was Christmas Day. All over London fathers with a grimly determined air were sharpening carving knives

and mothers were calling their toy-bloated children
to table.

In Hoxton Auntie Ringer's board groaned with the best
in the land, and the table was littered with a line of crackers
that Auntie could have sold at one and twopence a box easy,
if she'd had the mind to. Not that Auntie Ringer had
considered it for a moment. On Christmas Day your own
children came first.

The boys had gorged themselves into tight little drums,
and even Baby had eaten far more than any baby should.
But little Maudie was listless. She had finished up her turkey,
but she had not asked for a second helping and she was
toying—yes, that was the word—toying with her brandy
sauce.

'Now, Maudie,' said Auntie Ringer, 'eat up your nice
mince-pie. And enjoy it,' she ordered.

Maudie swallowed obediently. How tired she was. But
tired out or not, she was going out that afternoon—same
time, same place—to be given the present she had been
promised. It was ever so nice to be given a present by
someone you didn't expect a present from!

'Now, Maudie,' said Auntie Ringer, 'stop dreaming
whatever you're dreaming about and pull your cracker . . .'

Christmas afternoon. Same time. Same place. And there
was the tramp, by this time a little in love with his gift
himself. He kept taking it out of its box, pulling the strings
and listening fondly.

'You're a toff,' he kept assuring it.

And soon along came Maudie.

'Good afternoon,' she said politely. 'A Merry
Christmas.'

'Same to you, matey,' said the tramp. 'Did they feed you up all right?'

Maudie nodded. 'I brought you a present,' she said. 'Look!' She extended a pair of cuff links. 'They're real bone,' she pointed out.

'Coo,' said the tramp. 'Just what I been wanting.' He thrust out his frayed shirt cuffs. He donned the links complacently.

'They look ever so nice,' said Maudie a little uncertainly.

'That they do,' said the tramp. He shot them.

There was a satisfied silence.

'And now, matey,' said the tramp. 'I got something for you. And if you don't like it I'll eat my—cuff links!' he substituted.

It couldn't be! Maudie tore open the box. It was! . . . Maudie's eyes filled with tears.

'It says "Pa-pa" and "Ma-ma," ' said the tramp proudly. He showed her.

The little girl looked at the hated doll. She looked at the tramp, so kind, so happy and so expectant.

'It's ever so nice,' faltered Auntie Ringer's Maudie.

The tramp remembered the smile she had given him long after she had gone. Why, the little nipper was so happy there were tears in her eyes. It was good to make people happy at Christmas. Maybe, thought the tramp, looking into the comfortably distant future, he'd do another day's work next year.

And now Christmas Day was drawing to a surfeited close. All over London children were being told it was time to go to bed. But there had been no need to tell little Maudie this. She was already under her patchwork quilt, her teeth brushed, her prayers said, and her hair brushed and combed.

And there she lay, hugging the Paris doll. And even as her sleepy eyes closed, one arm tugged tenderly at the strings.

'Ma-ma,' said the doll. 'Pa . . .'

It was ever such a nice doll really, when you didn't have to sell it!

'Well, knock me down with a feather!' exclaimed Auntie Ringer when she bustled in to call Maudie next morning.

But since nobody in Hoxton would dare to attempt it, here our story ends.

The Old Pro

I T'S lovely money,' tempted the Agent.

'If it's there,' said the Old Pro gloomily.

Both took time off to greet the American girl who had made such a success in what was the thing called? The American girl, who had made such a success in etc., and couldn't place either of them, chatted cordially back for a few moments before hipping her way onwards to her window table at the Savoy.

The Grill was at its most elegant, as it always is after a first night. Seven interceptions, including Emlyn, and Luigi with her all the way. Maybe he was still trying to make up for the first time when, forgivably enough, mistaking her for just another American, he had handed her over to an underling. She leant back and loosened her minks. How soothing the Savoy was—when they liked you. It must be the carpet. Or the comfortable buzz of conversation, as well-known enemies greeted well-known enemies and made amusing remarks about mutual well-known enemies. just out of earshot, no doubt at that moment making amusing remarks about them. So much gayer than the Ivy where the tables were too close together to do that sort of thing—much. Though, mind you, the Ivy had something. Could it be the food?

'How are you, darling?' said Larry blondly.

'Oh, I'm grand,' said the American girl who had made such a success.

Soothing—that's what the Savoy was. Maybe it was the mirrors. She looked into the one beside her. Just a Broadway Broad, same as she'd always been—but a wow in London, Eng. Maybe it was the orchids.

An English Rose, fresh from an enthusiastic first night reception in a musical fated to come off next week, was making a triumphant entrance escorted by her husband, her lover, and his wife, and being led to a long thin table where the Backer and his two-line Baskova were already drinking.

The Agent and the Old Pro took time off to greet the procession.

'Six weeks?' suggested the Agent after they had passed.

'A fortnight,' said the Old Pro, who had seen the dress rehearsal. 'At the outside,' he added. He applied himself to his beer.

'Now look here, Clarrie,' said the Agent. 'I want you to have confidence in me. Haven't I always looked after you? Didn't I draw up your first contract?'

'And a lousy contract it was,' said Old Pro.

Conway Peake ignored this. 'Haven't I pushed you, built you up, made you what you are to-day? Have you ever taken my advice and regretted it?'

'Blackpool,' said the Old Pro.

'Was I to know the war was over?' said the Agent. He laughed. The Old Pro didn't.

'Anyway,' said the Agent, 'I'm asking you to have confidence in me now. I tell you these boys are all right. I'm not saying they're H. M. Tennant—yet—but they will be. I got confidence in them

'H'm,' said the Old Pro.

'They got enterprise. They got vision. And they got Hermione Baddeley.'

'Have they got any money?' asked the Old Pro.

'Could they hope to get Hermione without it?' said the Agent. 'Be your age. I tell you this management is all right. What's more,' he said in awe, 'they're honest—or one of them is.'

'Which one?' asked the Old Pro.

'Now look here, Clarrie,' said the Agent, who'd stood enough of this for ten per cent. 'You've come to a very critical point in your career. Either you're going to the top or you're going to the bottom. You're not getting younger, Clarrie, and you can't keep on playing the same parts over and over again. You're getting old, Clarrie, and you might as well face it.'

The Old Pro nodded gloomily.

'You got to do something different and this musical's your chance. I want you to consider it very seriously.'

The Old Pro considered it. 'Who's playing the lead if they don't hope for Hermione?'

'Mellow Marshmallow,' said the Agent smugly. He was her agent.

'Christ!' said the Old Pro.

'You can't talk like that about an artiste who's getting a hundred and twenty a week or eight and a half per cent., whichever is the greater,' said the Agent complacently.

'God! Is that what you swung on them?' asked the Old Pro.

The Agent lit a cigar. It was a sufficient answer. But it failed to silence the Old Pro.

'If Mellow's getting a hundred and twenty,' he announced, 'you'll get me seventy-five or I won't even look at it.'

'You'll be getting that and more,' said the Agent. 'Soon. Leave that side of it to me.'

He opened his brief-case and passed over a tattered script. It was headed 'Annie in Oklahoma.'

'Take it back and have a look at it, Clarrie,' he urged. 'And whatever you think of it, remember it ran for four years on Broadway.'

'So what,' said the Old Pro. With experienced fingers he thumbed through his part.

'First entrance weak,' he said. 'I fizzle out in the second half.' He thumbed on. 'Not on in the finale! Hey—what are you trying to sell me?'

'How can you be on in the finale when you've just been killed,' said the Agent.

'On or off?' asked the Old Pro.

'On, of course,' said the Agent. 'What d'you think I am?'

'Oh!' said the Old Pro. 'How long do I take to die?'

'Quite a time,' said the Agent.

'Ah,' said the Old Pro. He began to thumb his way back through the pages.

'It hasn't been rewritten yet,' said the Agent quickly. 'You see it was going to be quite a small part at first.'

'So I notice,' said the Old Pro, still thumbing.

'But if you're going to do it they'll want to build it up. What do you think they'll pay seventy-five a week for? It's lovely money,' tempted the Agent.

'If it's there,' said the Old Pro.

They were back where we came in.

Luigi came floating along solicitously ushering an ensemble of dessicated charm topped off by a wilting carnation. It was Harridine Representation Inc.—in person.

'Hallo, Skinny,' said Conway Peake. 'How did it go?'

'Fine,' said Harridine without conviction. 'Besides,' he added, 'I'm in on the film rights, and what's more,' he came half alive, 'I'm going to sell them to-night.' He stiffened what there was of his chin and marched off to join a table that appeared to contain Alexander Korda, Emeric Pressburger, Sydney Box, Micky Balcon, Lou Jackson, J. Arthur Rank and Poppa Somlo. At the next table a shape that appeared to be that of Del Giudice seemed to be laughing its head off.

'About this proposition, Clarrie,' said the Agent. 'I want you to consider it seriously—dead seriously. And while you're considering it I'll draw up the contract.'

'It'd mean missing the Panto season,' said the Old Pro, 'and Mum won't like that.'

'What is it this year?' asked the Agent. 'Cinderella at Newcastle?'

'Puss in Boots at Bradford,' said the Old Pro. 'You know, Con, it's funny, but I've never played in Puss.'

'Too bad,' said the Agent. 'Well, your Mum will have to get along without you this year. She'll manage all right.' He grinned.

'I don't see much of Mum as things are,' said the Old Pro. 'I like spending Christmas with the old geezer. She knows more about the show business than both the Littlers put together, and,' he looked round the tables, 'Bernie Delfont thrown in for luck. Besides, it's my birthday on New Year's Eve. Did I ever tell you,' he asked, 'that I was born in a dressing-room in the middle of Robinson Crusoe? The star's dressing-room,' he swanked.

'Sure you were,' said the Agent.

'On New Year's Eve when the bells were ringing,' said the Old Pro with a sudden softness in his face. 'Ma's understudy played for her in the second half. Ruby Rubarto. She flopped,' he remembered with satisfaction.

'This year you'll be spending your birthday up in lights in the West End of London—with luck,' said the Agent. 'How old will you be, Clarrie?' he asked.

'Twelve,' said the Old Pro firmly.

'Come, come,' said Conway Peake reproachfully. 'Mustn't lie to your agent.'

The Old Pro stubbed his sulky cigarette on a Savoy saucer.

'All right,' he said, 'if you must have it—fourteen.'

Luigi came floating along solicitously ushering a brilliantly brilliantined small boy, who had just taken London by storm in A Sinner on Sunday. The small boy turned his freckles on the Old Pro as he passed.

'Why, Clarrie?' he said. 'What are you doing here? Give my regards to your Mum.' He passed on to exchange a wisecrack with Bea Lillie. He got the worst of that one.

'Blast him,' said the Old Pro. 'Patronizing me just because he's two years younger!'

*   *   *   *   *

The 'Annie in Oklahoma' company was standing in a knot on Euston station. It was high summer. It was freezing. They were opening the day after to-morrow in Edinburgh and the costumes hadn't come. Almost it might have been 'A Bullet in the Ballet.'

Around them, like a distracted nursemaid moth, fluttered Arundel of Isaacs, Cohen and Arundel, the enterprising management that was not H. M. Tennant yet. He fussed, he flurried, he assured everybody that everything would be all right, and he tugged ineffectually at the locked handles on the carriages reserved for the company to the evident amusement of Messrs. Isaacs and Cohen, who, having meanly got on the train lower down, had bribed their way through and were comfortably ensconced each in his corner seat. So was the Old Pro, who had done exactly the same thing, except that he had hurried along behind them and saved himself the bribing.

'Hey, Clarrie,' called Conway Peake, who though he had no intention of going all that way North to see an opening in which only two of his clients were involved, had nevertheless come to the station to make certain they embarked, 'save a seat for Miss Marshmallow, will you?'

Christ! thought the Old Pro. He leant out of the window. 'Sure, Mellow,' he said. 'Right next to me. We might play some gin rummy,' he suggested.

'Oh no we won't,' said Miss Mellow Marshmallow with all the usual acumen of the extremely blonde.

The fussing Arundel had at last triumphantly collected a guard to unlock the doors. He had been on his way to do it, anyway. The company bundled in, the nippier chorus, as usual, beating the less nimble principals to the corner seats, and leaving Rickie Ricardo, the golden-voiced tenor, to stand coldly in the corridor with a disconcerted Backer, at the beginning of a series of disbeliefs that things like this could happen to him. A great sense of humour Messrs. Isaacs and Cohen had, though of course Arundel must be made to give up his seat presently. A Backer must be comfortable. Not to mention that the chance of a little poker game mustn't be missed.

In front of the coach fond mothers were saying good-bye to their daughters and gazing enviously at other fond mothers travelling North with their daughters.

'Well, well, well,' said Conway Peake. 'Look after yourself Mellow and keep Clarrie away from the drink. You're off now.'

This time he was right.

'Thank God for that,' said the Old Pro. He took off his coat and put it neatly on the rack. He opened his valise and produced a tiny portable radio, a copy of the *New Yorker*, and an air cushion. He blew up the cushion and tucked it behind him. He took off his shoes and put on his bedroom slippers. He wrapped a camel-hair rug round himself and turned on the radio. He opened a zip bag and pulled out a thermos and some paper containers.

'Cup of tea,' he offered hospitably.

'Thanks,' said Miss Marshmallow.

'Slab of chocolate?'

'Thanks,' said Miss Marshmallow.

'Sardine on biscuit?' The Old Pro went to work with a tin opener.

'My God,' said Miss Marshmallow, 'you do think of everything!'

'Oh, it's nothing,' said the Old Pro. 'Just the way I was brought up.'

*   *   *   *   *

'Yes, Mellow,' the Old Pro was saying. 'I always used to enjoy Little Willie. You don't get parts like that at my age.'

Miss Marshmallow inspected her stretched-out nylons. 'Oh, I don't know,' she said.

'That's just it,' said the Old Pro. 'You don't know. You people that didn't join the profession till you were in your graves.' He looked forlornly out of the window, regretting his maturity. 'It's awful to think that all my best parts are behind me,' he mourned.

'Cheer up,' said Miss Marshmallow unimpressed. 'There's still Peter Pan.'

The Old Pro considered it. 'Dogs and kids always steal a show—no matter how small the part is. And if you give them anything to do—well, the rest of us might as well not be on. Shall I tell you a bad dream of mine?' he asked. 'It's playing Grandad to someone else's little Lord Fauntleroy. Been getting it twice a year since I was eleven. Poor Aubrey,' he said inconsequently.

'Sometimes I dream I'm Lilian Braithwaite,' said Miss Marshmallow. She leant back and closed her eyes and the daylight searched out every one of the lines that six weeks of hard rehearsing had planted on her twenty-nine-year-old face.

'First luncheon ready,' intoned the attendant, swaying down the corridor.

Messrs. Isaacs and Cohen rose from their corner seats.

'Lunch tickets?' They stretched out their hands to Arundel.

'Good God,' said Arundel guiltily.

They cursed him.

But in the Old Pro's compartment a chicken was being torn comfortably to pieces, and a bottle of Algerian was pretending it was every bit as good as a Pommard. There was also a Camembert cheese, two oranges, and brandy in a silver travelling flask.

'A present from Mum on my ninth birthday,' said the Old Pro pointing to it.

'I'll say one thing for you,' conceded Miss Marshmallow. 'You may be a pest at rehearsals, but you do things in style all right. Where are you staying? The Caledonian?'

'God, no,' said the Old Pro. 'I haven't stayed at a hotel

since I was six. Digs for me every time. I've got a way with landladies,' he said modestly.

'You can get a room with a bath at the Caledonian,' said Miss Marshmallow.

'They warm the bath-water for me of an evening at my digs—when I want it,' said the Old Pro. 'And they cook me a hot supper—when I want it. And they cook what I want—when I want it.'

'Where?' asked Miss Marshmallow.

'Oh, everywhere,' said the Old Pro. 'There isn't an A date in England where there isn't a landlady with a photograph of me on her mantelpiece. At Edinburgh, it's Mrs. Macgillicuddy, No. 17, the Crescent. Know her?' he asked.

'No,' said Miss Marshmallow crisply.

'Pity,' said the Old Pro. 'There's not many like Ma Macgillicuddy left these days. She knows how to look after people like us. And she's a good judge of a show too. If Ma likes us on Monday night, we'll be all right.' He shook his head. 'Not that she will,' he said gloomily.

Miss Marshmallow was alarmed. 'You don't mean that, Clarrie,' she said. 'Why, everyone says it's going to be a wonderful show.'

'That's bad,' said the Old Pro judiciously. 'Mind you,' he admitted, 'the show's there all right if we stay out long enough to get at it. But it's not there yet and the way this management is setting about things . . .'

'Give them a chance,' said Miss Marshmallow. 'They're new.'

*   *   *   *   *

The new management arrived at Waverley station to be greeted by no porters. It was Sunday. But the scenery for

'Annie in Oklahoma' couldn't stay in the van till Monday.

'You see to it,' said Cohen and Isaacs to Arundel. They made off in the direction of the only taxi, but were beaten to it by the Old Pro.

'In with you Mellow, my girl,' the Old Pro was ordering, 'before they call for volunteers for the unloading.'

As they rounded the corner they caught a fascinating glimpse of a shirt-sleeved Arundel trying to persuade the Backer to give a hand.

'Call this a management,' sniffed the Old Pro. 'Didn't even know there were no porters at Waverley on Sundays.'

'Give them a chance,' said Miss Marshmallow. 'They're new.'

'The trouble about being new,' said the Old Pro, 'is that you think you know it all.'

Miss Marshmallow looked out of the window on Sunday night at Edinburgh. 'They got vision,' she argued.

'Who told you that?' asked the Old Pro. 'Con? Well, take it from me that their idea of vision is saving a penny in the wrong place. Why aren't we travelling an orchestra? Who's building our scenery? Ever heard of them? And they tell me the ballet haven't seen their costumes yet. Believe me,' he said, 'there's going to be trouble at the dress rehearsal.'

* * * * *

Believe us, there was.

Arundel, pink as a baby and far more hopeful, arriving at the theatre refreshed by a night's sleep and all set for a series of breezy 'Hello, my dears,' and quite a bit of bottom-pinching, found the stage full of a livid corps-de-ballet, tugging at tight shoulders and loose waists with one needlewoman trying to attend to the lot of them.

'The costumes have come,' he guessed.

'They don't fit,' complained Cohen.

'And we've paid for them,' wailed Isaacs. 'Most of them.'

'Mr. Arundel!' An excited dragoon blew his chest out. A button popped. 'How can I dance in this?' He raised his arms above his head. The jacket rose with them.

'Mr. Arundel! Mr. Arundel!' The entire corps-de-ballet came surging round, each displaying her particular misfit and leaving a staggering total to be put right, if possible, by to-night, or, at any rate, less wrong.

'See to it, Arundel,' said Isaacs and Cohen. They made off.

Arundel, helpless amid the storm, sighted the needle-woman.

'Maggie!' he appealed. 'Do something!'

'I am doing something,' said Maggie. She went on stitching at the lowest wave of the sea of garments flung at her by the infuriated sylphs.

'Can't you get some help?' bleated Arundel.

'In Edinburgh?' said Maggie. She went on stitching.

'Oh dear,' said Arundel. He looked round for comfort. He spotted a group of carpenters hammering above the stage manager's shouting. 'Scenery here all right?' he called.

'It's here all right,' said the stage manager. 'But it doesn't fit. What's more,' he added, 'the transparency curtain is torn to ribbons.'

'Who tore it?' demanded Arundel. He looked round for a whipping boy.

There was a roar as of thunder. A trolley was being pushed on to the stage. On it was a marble staircase. It was swaying.

Rickie Ricardo came forward and gazed at it with growing disfavour.

'I'm not going to risk my golden voice on that," he pronounced. 'How are you going to keep it steady?'

'That's what I want to know,' said the head carpenter. 'I've been against these trolleys all along. They're no quicker than flying the stuff and twice the trouble.'

'And fifty times the noise,' said Miss Marshmallow.

'Hello, darling,' said Arundel with charm. 'Everything all right?'

'The trouble with you,' said Miss Marshmallow nastily, 'is that you're new.'

'Oh dear,' thought Arundel. Still, he comforted himself, it's always like this at dress rehearsals—so they say—'It'll be all right on the night,' he found himself announcing into a sudden silence.

The Old Pro strolled languidly on.

A whipping boy.

'You're late, Mr. Jones,' snapped Arundel. 'You were called for ten. Why weren't you here?'

'Be your age,' said the Old Pro. He turned a lack lustre eye on the pandemonium. 'You haven't even got as far as I expected. Morning, Maggie.' He dropped a kiss on the needlewoman's head. 'I've got you a tailor.'

'What in Edinburgh?' said Maggie.

'Friend of Ma Macgillicuddy's,' said the Old Pro. 'I've promised his family a box and he's sending his girls here right away. Double rates, of course, but that's the management's look out.'

'What's that?' said Isaacs and Cohen appearing suddenly.

'We've got to have it,' said Maggie firmly.

That settled the costumes—more or less. But the problems of the scenery that wouldn't fit, the transparency that was far too transparent, the noiseless trolley that sounded like the last trump and the augmented part-time orchestra that had never seen the score and wouldn't till the band parts were ready, which might be any time but wouldn't be soon, still remained. By late afternoon the new management was still struggling with these problems and not a single scene staged yet and a press party at the biggest hotel which nobody could attend.

'At this,' said Arundel, 'we'll never ring up to-night.'

'We will,' said the Old Pro confidently.

Cr-r-sh!

The truck with the marble staircase on it had broken loose and run over the only actor who had been rehearsed in the few simple steps that would enable him to appear with the ballet at a plot point in the play.

Arundel went mad. 'Doctor!' he screamed. 'Ambulance! Police!'

While he was still screaming the Old Pro had sent for the theatre doctor and gone into consultation with the producer who, so far, had been sitting in a stall in his overcoat waiting to produce.

'There's no one who can do it,' declared the producer. 'And there's no time to rehearse an understudy.'

'That settles it,' said Arundel in despair. 'We'll never ring up now.'

'Rubbish,' said the Old Pro. 'If we can't manage an understudy we'll alter the play. Where's that script?' He concentrated.

'What's the use,' said Arundel. 'I'd better ring up Moss Empires and ask for a postponement.'

'You won't get it,' said the Old Pro. He went back to the script. He concentrated. He closed it with a satisfied snap.

'Simple,' he said. 'We cut out the scene. The show's too long, anyway.'

'That's right,' said the producer. He brightened. 'Here, gimme that script.' He went to work with a blue pencil.

'Well,' said the stage manager. 'that's the best we can do for the moment.' He stepped back to admire A Sunset in Arizona. It was madly pink. He shuddered.

But the sight of a real piece of canvas actually set in place heartened Arundel. Now at last he felt he belonged to the theatre—that he was a part of the show business. And maybe, now, it *would* be all right on the night.

$$\star \qquad \star \qquad \star \qquad \star \qquad \star$$

The night. It was all right.

The curtain rose on time, or very nearly, even though it had been lowered hurriedly half an hour before to cut off a still-rehearsing company from a trickling-in audience.

But right from the start the show went over with a bang, including the very loud ones between scenes and behind tabs. That they drowned the dialogue spoken in front of them hardly mattered—it was too London, anyway. So were a great many of the laughs that missed fire. But there were Edinburgh laughs to compensate—for instance, the roar that rose when the marble staircase ran away with the golden voice and had to be pushed back again while it went on singing. And the rapturous whistles that greeted the villain who, fighting Annie for her honour in Oklahoma, found himself standing with an armful of come-to-pieces dress and gazing in horror at Annie in her underwear, a horror by no means shared by the audience.

'That's good,' said Isaacs.

'We'll keep it in,' said Cohen.

Then there was the Old Pro's death scene. It went well
but it wasn't Little Willie. Only four handkerchiefs came
out in the stalls, and two of them didn't count—they
belonged to Isaacs and Cohen. But of course he couldn't
see what was happening in the Gods. That's where he
always got 'em.

'Say good-bye to Annie for me,' he tremoloed, 'and tell
her . . . tell her . . .'

A roar of thunder drowned the message. The marble
staircase had got loose again. The golden-voiced tenor, this
time, at his own insistence, safely on the ground, jettisoned
his attitude of grief and smirked.

But the audience loved it. Ever since A Bullet in the Ballet
they expected a bit of fun on first nights in Edinburgh.

And so the evening jolted, crashed, warbled and thundered
its way to a triumphant finale. There were eleven curtain
calls and a call for an extra rehearsal at 10 a.m. to-morrow.
Miss Marshmallow, in her own dependable street suit said
that this was the happiest evening of her life and the audience
sounded as though it believed her.

And then the orchestra played them out of the theatre.

The company relaxed.

'We've done it,' gasped Arundel embracing Miss Marshmallow.

'We've done it,' sobbed Isaacs embracing Cohen.

'We've done it,' gloated the Backer embracing his little
Baskova.

But the Old Pro shook his head.

'It'll never get to London,' he said, and went off to 'phone
his Mum to tell her he'd be with her at Christmas in Puss in
Boots.

And he was.

The Man in the Snuff-Coloured Suit

THERE were six passengers in the third-class railway compartment: the Burly Man, the Observant Man, the Angry Man, the Man with the Cough, the Man with the Cold, and the Man in the Snuff-Coloured Suit— and they were reading: the *Greyhound Express*, the *Daily Express*, the *New Statesman*, the *New Leader*, and 'Who Killed the Count?' The Burly Man was absorbed, the Observant Man was looking out of the window, the Angry Man's veins were swelling visibly, the Man with the Cough coughed, the Man with the Cold kept blowing his nose, and the Man in the Snuff-Coloured Suit turned the pages of 'Who Killed the Count?' feverishly while his hair stood on end. It was clear that he hadn't the slightest idea.

The engine whistled. The train went into a tunnel. The compartment went black.

When it was light again the Man with the Cough had stopped coughing. He was lying on the floor with a knife in his back.

Five passengers rose as one. They bent over the body.

'Dead,' said the Observant Man.

'Kicked the bucket,' said the Burly Man.

'Stabbed in the back,' said the Man with the Cold.

'Now there'll be an inquest!' said the Angry Man.

'Oh, dear,' said the Man in the Snuff-Coloured Suit.

Five passengers looked at each other. Four passengers reached for the Communication cord.

'Wait!' said the Observant Man. He pointed to a notice. 'PENALTY FOR IMPROPER USE—£5,' it read.

Four passengers thought better of it.

His authority established, the Observant Man put himself in charge.

'Everybody stay where you are,' he said needlessly. 'This is a murder and one of us is a killer. We are all,' he pointed out gravely, 'under equal suspicion.'

The Angry Man rounded on him.

'Does this mean, sir,' he demanded, 'that you suspect me?'

The Man with the Cold sneezed.

'Murder or no murder, I'm not missing the first race at White City,' said the Burly Man. He brandished his *Greyhound Express*.

'Oh, dear,' said the Man in the Snuff-Coloured Suit.

The Observant Man silenced them all with a gesture.

'One of us is a killer,' he resumed. 'We all had the opportunity. One of us had the means.' He pointed starkly to the knife. 'It should be possible by a simple process of elimination . . .'

The engine whistled. The train went into a tunnel. The compartment went dark.

When it was light again the Observant Man was lying beside the Man with the Cough. A knife was sticking in his back.

The elimination seemed to have started.

'Now look here,' said the Angry Man, 'this is getting beyond a joke.'

'I'll say it is,' agreed the Burly Man.

'Oh, dear,' said the Man in the Snuff-Coloured Suit.

The Man with the Cold gazed fascinated at the bodies.

'Are there any more tunnels on this line?' he asked, worried.

The engine whistled. The compartment went black.

When it was light again the Man with the Cold was lying on the floor with a knife in his back.

The Angry Man controlled himself with a mighty effort.

'Three of us left,' he said, 'and one of us a killer. I put it to you, gentlemen, that the two innocent men must combine to protect themselves against the guilty.'

The engine whistled. The compartment went black.

When it was light again it was evident that they hadn't. Only two men left alive!

The Burly Man advanced on the Man in the Snuff-Coloured Suit.

'Well, old cock,' he said, 'this makes things simple. Either you did it or,' he came closer, 'I did.'

'Oh, dear,' said the Man in the Snuff-Coloured Suit. He backed.

The Burly Man followed and stuck out his chin.

'Well,' he demanded. 'Is it You or Me?'

The engine whistled. The compartment went black.

When it was light again the Man in the Snuff-Coloured Suit stood looking down at five backs with five knives in them. 'Who Killed the Count?' fluttered from his hands.

'Oh, dear,' he said. 'It must be me.'